DOVER · THRIFT · EDITIONS

The Nutcracker
and
The Golden Pot

E. T. A. HOFFMANN

DOVER PUBLICATIONS, INC.
New York

DOVER THRIFT EDITIONS

GENERAL EDITOR: STANLEY APPELBAUM
EDITOR OF THIS VOLUME: PHILIP SMITH

COPYRIGHT

Published in Canada by General Publishing Company, Ltd., 30 Lesmill Road, Don Mills, Toronto, Ontario.

Published in the United Kingdom by Constable and Company, Ltd., 3 The Lanchesters, 162–164 Fulham Palace Road, London W6 9ER.

BIBLIOGRAPHICAL NOTE

This Dover edition, first published in 1993, contains unabridged reprints of two works from *The Best Tales of Hoffmann*, first published by Dover Publications, Inc., in 1967 (see the introductory Note, specially prepared for the present edition, for further details on the translations).

LIBRARY OF CONGRESS CATALOGING-IN-PUBLICATION DATA

Hoffmann, E. T. A. (Ernst Theodor Amadeus), 1776–1822.
   [Nussknacker und Mausekönig.   English]
   The nutcracker and The golden pot / E. T. A. Hoffmann.
       p.   cm. — (Dover thrift editions)
   ISBN 0-486-27806-9
   I. Hoffmann, E. T. A. (Ernst Theodor Amadeus), 1776–1822.
Goldne Topf. English. 1993. II. Title. III. Series.
PT2361.E5N87   1993
833'.6—dc20   93–4884
                                    CIP

Manufactured in the United States of America
Dover Publications, Inc., 31 East 2nd Street, Mineola, N.Y. 11501

Note

"The Nutcracker" and "The Golden Pot" are the best-known and the most highly regarded, respectively, of the tales of Ernst Theodor Amadeus Hoffmann (1776–1822). One of the outstanding figures of German Romanticism, Hoffmann was an active writer, composer, conductor, music critic and artist; his stories, which brought him his greatest success, reflect the breadth of his interests, and have served as the inspiration for important works such as Offenbach's opera *Les contes d'Hoffmann* and Tchaikovsky's ballet *Shchelkunchik* [*The Nutcracker*]. Hoffmann's flair for the grotesque and fantastical was also an acknowledged influence on writers such as Carlyle, Poe and Baudelaire.

The texts used in this volume are taken from *The Best Tales of Hoffmann* [Dover 0-486-21793-0], edited by E. F. Bleiler. "The Golden Pot" is a slightly revised version of Carlyle's translation of "Der goldne Topf," which first appeared in his *German Romance* (1827). "The Nutcracker" is a slightly revised version of Major Alexander Ewing's translation of "Nussknacker und Mausekönig."

Contents

The Golden Pot

FIRST VIGIL

On Ascension Day, about three o'clock in the afternoon in Dresden, a young man dashed through the Schwarzthor, or Black Gate, and ran right into a basket of apples and cookies which an old and very ugly woman had set out for sale. The crash was prodigious; what wasn't squashed or broken was scattered, and hordes of street urchins delightedly divided the booty which this quick gentleman had provided for them. At the fearful shrieking which the old hag began, her fellow vendors, leaving their cake and brandy tables, surrounded the young man, and with plebian violence scolded and stormed at him. For shame and vexation he uttered no word, but merely held out his small and by no means particularly well-filled purse, which the old woman eagerly seized and stuck into her pocket.

The hostile ring of bystanders now broke; but as the young man started off, the hag called after him, "Ay, run, run your way, Devil's Bird! You'll end up in the crystal! The crystal!" The screeching harsh voice of the woman had something unearthly in it: so that the promenaders paused in amazement, and the laughter, which at first had been universal, instantly died away. The Student Anselmus, for the young man was no other, even though he did not in the least understand these singular phrases, felt himself seized with a certain involuntary horror; and he quickened his steps still more, until he was almost running, to escape the curious looks of the multitude, all of whom were staring at him. As he made his way through the crowd of well-dressed people, he heard them muttering on all sides: "Poor young fellow! Ha! What a vicious old witch!" The mysterious words of the old woman, oddly enough, had given this ludicrous adventure a sort of sinister turn; and the youth, previously unobserved, was now regarded with a certain sympathy. The ladies, because of his fine figure and handsome face, which the glow of inward anger rendered still more expressive, forgave him his awkwardness, as well as the dress he

1

wore, though it was at variance with all fashion. His pike-gray frock was shaped as if the tailor had known the modern style only by hearsay; and his well-kept black satin trousers gave him a certain pedagogic air, to which his gait and manner did not at all correspond.

The Student had almost reached the end of the alley which leads out to the Linkische Bath; but his breath could no longer stand such a pace. From running, he took to walking; but he still hardly dared to lift an eye from the ground, for he still saw apples and cookies dancing around him, and every kind look from this or that pretty girl seemed to him to be only a continuation of the mocking laughter at the Schwarzthor.

In this mood he reached the entrance of the Bath: groups of holiday people, one after the other, were moving in. Music of wind instruments resounded from the place, and the din of merry guests was growing louder and louder. The poor Student Anselmus was almost ready to weep; since Ascension Day had always been a family festival for him, he had hoped to participate in the felicities of the Linkische paradise; indeed, he had intended even to go to the length of a half portion of coffee with rum and a whole bottle of double beer, and he had put more money in his purse than was entirely convenient or advisable. And now, by accidentally kicking the apple-and-cookie basket, he had lost all the money he had with him. Of coffee, of double or single beer, of music, of looking at the pretty girls—in a word, of all his fancied enjoyments there was now nothing more to be said. He glided slowly past; and at last turned down the Elbe road, which at that time happened to be quite empty.

Beneath an elder-tree, which had grown out through the wall, he found a kind green resting place: here he sat down, and filled a pipe from the Sanitätsknaster, or health-tobacco-box, of which his friend the Conrector Paulmann had lately made him a present. Close before him rolled and chafed the gold-dyed waves of the fair Elbe: on the other side rose lordly Dresden, stretching, bold and proud, its light towers into the airy sky; farther off, the Elbe bent itself down towards flowery meads and fresh springing woods; and in the dim distance, a range of azure peaks gave notice of remote Bohemia. But, heedless of this, the Student Anselmus, looking gloomily before him, blew forth smoky clouds into the air. His chagrin at length became audible, and he said, "In truth, I am born to losses and crosses for all my life! That, as a boy, I could never guess the right way at Odds and Evens; that my bread and butter always fell on the buttered side—but I won't even mention these sorrows. But now that I've become a student, in spite of Satan, isn't it a frightful fate that I'm still as bumbling as ever? Can I put on a new coat without getting grease on it the first day, or without tearing a cursed hole in it on some nail or other? Can I ever bow to a Councillor or a lady without pitching the hat out of my hands, or even slipping on the smooth pavement, and taking an embarrassing fall? When I was in Halle, didn't I have to pay three or four groschen every market day for broken crockery—the Devil putting it into my head to dash straight forward like a lemming? Have I ever got to my college, or any other place that I had an appointment to, at the right time? Did it ever matter if I set out a half hour early, and planted myself at the door, with the knocker in my hand? Just as the clock is going to strike, souse! Some devil empties a wash basin down on me, or I run into some fellow coming out, and get myself engaged in endless quarrels until the time is clean gone.

"Ah, well. Where are you fled now, you blissful dreams of coming fortune, when I proudly thought that I might even reach the height of Geheimrat? And hasn't my evil star estranged me from my best patrons? I had heard, for instance, that the Councillor, to whom I have a letter of introduction, cannot stand hair cut close; with an immensity of trouble the barber managed to fasten a little queue to the back of my head; but at my first bow his unblessed knot comes loose, and a little dog which had been snuffing around me frisks off to the Geheimrat with the queue in its mouth. I spring after it in terror, and stumble against the table, where he has been working while at breakfast; and cups, plates, ink-glass, sandbox crash to the floor and a flood of chocolate and ink covers the report he has just been writing. 'Is the Devil in this man?' bellows the furious Privy Councillor, and he shoves me out of the room.

"What did it matter when Conrector Paulmann gave me hopes of copywork: will the malignant fate, which pursues me everywhere, permit it? Today even! Think of it! I intended to celebrate Ascension Day with cheerfulness of soul. I was going to stretch a point for once. I might have gone, as well as anyone else, into the Linkische Bath, and called out proudly, 'Marqueur, a bottle of double beer; best sort, if you please.' I might have sat till far in the evening; and moreover close by this or that fine party of well-dressed ladies. I know it, I feel it! Heart would have come into me, I should have been quite another man; nay, I might have carried it so far, that when one of them asked, 'What time is it?' or 'What is it they are playing?' I would have started up with light grace, and without overturning my glass, or stumbling over the bench, but with a graceful bow, moving a step and a half forward, I would have answered, 'Give me leave, mademoiselle! it is the overture of the *Donauweibchen*'; or, 'It is just going to strike six.' Could any mortal in the world have taken it ill of me? No! I say; the girls would have looked over, smiling so roguishly; as they always do when I pluck up heart to show them that I too understand the light tone of society, and know how ladies should be spoken to. And now the Devil himself leads me into that cursed apple-basket, and now I must sit moping in solitude, with nothing but a poor pipe of——" Here the Student Anselmus was interrupted in his soliloquy by a strange rustling and whisking, which rose close by him in the grass, but soon glided up into the twigs and leaves of the elder-tree that stretched out over his head. It was as if the evening wind were shaking the leaves, as if little birds were twittering among the branches, moving their little wings in capricious flutter to and fro. Then he heard a whispering and lisping, and it seemed as if the blossoms were sounding like little crystal bells. Anselmus listened and listened. Ere long, the whispering, and lisping, and tinkling, he himself knew not how, grew to faint and half-scattered words:

"'Twixt this way, 'twixt that; 'twixt branches, 'twixt blossoms, come shoot, come twist and twirl we! Sisterkin, sisterkin! up to the shine; up, down, through and through, quick! Sunrays yellow; evening wind whispering; dewdrops pattering; blossoms all singing: sing we with branches and blossoms! Stars soon glitter; must down: 'twixt this way, 'twixt that, come shoot, come twist, come twirl we, sisterkin!"

And so it went along, in confused and confusing speech. The Student Anselmus thought: "Well, it is only the evening wind, which tonight truly is whispering distinctly enough." But at that moment there sounded over his head, as it were, a triple harmony of clear crystal bells: he looked up, and perceived three little snakes, glittering with green and gold, twisted around the branches, and stretching out their heads to the evening sun. Then, again, began a whispering and twittering in the same words as before, and the little snakes went gliding and caressing up and down through the twigs; and while they moved so rapidly, it was as if the elder-bush were scattering a thousand glittering emeralds through the dark leaves.

"It is the evening sun sporting in the elder-bush," thought the Student Anselmus; but the bells sounded again; and Anselmus observed that one snake held out its little head to him. Through all his limbs there went a shock like electricity; he quivered in his inmost heart: he kept gazing up, and a pair of glorious dark-blue eyes were looking at him with unspeakable longing; and an unknown feeling of highest blessedness and deepest sorrow nearly rent his heart asunder. And as he looked, and still looked, full of warm desire, into those kind eyes, the crystal bells sounded louder in harmonious accord, and the glittering emeralds fell down and encircled him, flickering round him in a thousand sparkles and sporting in resplendent threads of gold. The elder-bush moved and spoke: "You lay in my shadow; my perfume flowed around you, but you understood it not. The perfume is my speech, when love kindles it." The evening wind came gliding past, and said: "I played round your temples, but you understood me not. That breath is my speech, when love kindles it." The sunbeam broke through the clouds, and the sheen of it burned, as in words: "I over-flowed you, with glowing gold, but you understood me not. That glow is my speech, when love kindles it."

And, still deeper and deeper sank in the view of those glorious eyes, his longing grew keener, his desire more warm. And all rose and moved around him, as if awakening to glad life. Flowers and blossoms shed their odours round him, and their odour was like the lordly singing of a thousand softest voices, and what they sang was borne, like an echo, on the golden evening clouds, as they flitted away, into far-off lands. But as the last sunbeam abruptly sank behind the hills, and the twilight threw its veil over the scene, there came a hoarse deep voice, as from a great distance:

"Hey! hey! what chattering and jingling is that up there? Hey! hey! who catches me the ray behind the hills? Sunned enough, sung enough. Hey! hey! through bush and grass, through grass and stream. Hey! hey! Come dow-w-n, dow-w-w-n!"

So the voice faded away, as in murmurs of a distant thunder; but the crystal bells broke off in sharp discords. All became mute; and the Student Anselmus observed how the three snakes, glittering and sparkling, glided through the grass towards the river; rustling and hustling, they rushed into the Elbe; and over the waves where they vanished, there crackled up a green flame, which, gleaming forward obliquely, vanished in the direction of the city.

SECOND VIGIL

"The gentleman is ill?" said a decent burgher's wife, who, returning from a walk with her family, had paused here, and, with

crossed arms, was looking at the mad pranks of the Student Anselmus. Anselmus had clasped the trunk of the elder-tree, and was
calling incessantly up to the branches and leaves: "O glitter and
shine once more, dear gold snakes: let me hear your little bell-
voices once more! Look on me once more, kind eyes; O once, or I
must die in pain and warm longing!" And with this, he was
sighing and sobbing from the bottom of his heart most pitifully; and
in his eagerness and impatience, shaking the elder-tree to and fro;
which, however, instead of any reply, rustled quite stupidly and
unintelligibly with its leaves; and so rather seemed, as it were, to
make sport of the Student Anselmus and his sorrows.

"The gentleman is ill!" said the burgher's wife; and Anselmus
felt as if someone had shaken him out of a deep dream, or poured
ice-cold water on him, to awaken him without loss of time. He now
first saw clearly where he was, and recollected what a strange
apparition had assaulted him, nay, so beguiled his senses, as to make
him break forth into loud talk with himself. In astonishment, he
gazed at the woman, and at last snatching up his hat, which had
fallen to the ground in his transport, was about to make off in all
speed. The burgher himself had come forward in the meanwhile,
and, setting down the child from his arm on the grass, had been
leaning on his staff, and with amazement listening and looking at
the Student. He now picked up the pipe and tobacco-box which
the Student had let fall, and, holding them out to him, said:
"Don't take on so dreadfully, my worthy sir, or alarm people in the
dark, when nothing is the matter, after all, but a drop or two of
christian liquor: go home, like a good fellow, and sleep it off."

The Student Anselmus felt exceedingly ashamed; he uttered
nothing but a most lamentable Ah!

"Pooh! Pooh!" said the burgher, "never mind it a jot; such a
thing will happen to the best; on good old Ascension Day a man
may readily enough forget himself in his joy, and gulp down a
thought too much. A clergyman himself is no worse for it: I
presume, my worthy sir, you are a *Candidatus*. But, with your
leave, sir, I shall fill my pipe with your tobacco; mine was used up
a little while ago."

This last sentence the burgher uttered while the Student Anselmus
was about to put away his pipe and box; and now the burgher
slowly and deliberately cleaned his pipe, and began as slowly to fill
it. Several burgher girls had come up: these were speaking secretly
with the woman and each other, and tittering as they looked at
Anselmus. The Student felt as if he were standing on prickly

thorns, and burning needles.   No sooner had he got back his pipe and tobacco-box, than he darted off as fast as he could.

All the strange things he had seen were clean gone from his memory; he simply recollected having babbled all sorts of foolish stuff beneath the elder-tree.   This was the more frightful to him, as he entertained an inward horror against all soliloquists.   It is Satan that chatters out of them, said his Rector; and Anselmus had honestly believed him.   But to be regarded as a *Candidatus Theologiæ*, overtaken with drink on Ascension Day!   The thought was intolerable.

Running on with these mad vexations, he was just about turning up Poplar Alley, by the Kosel garden, when a voice behind him called out: "Herr Anselmus!   Herr Anselmus! for the love of Heaven, where are you running in such a hurry?"   The Student paused, as if rooted to the ground; for he was convinced that now some new accident would befall him.   The voice rose again: "Herr Anselmus, come back: we are waiting for you here at the water!"   And now the Student perceived that it was his friend Conrector Paulmann's voice: he went back to the Elbe, and found the Conrector, with his two daughters, as well as Registrator Heerbrand, all about to step into their gondola.   Conrector Paulmann invited the Student to go with them across the Elbe, and then to pass the evening at his house in the suburb of Pirna.   The Student Anselmus very gladly accepted this proposal, thinking thereby to escape the malignant destiny which had ruled over him all day.

Now, as they were crossing the river, it chanced that on the farther bank in Anton's Garden, some fireworks were just going off.   Sputtering and hissing, the rockets went aloft, and their blazing stars flew to pieces in the air, scattering a thousand vague shoots and flashes around them.   The Student Anselmus was sitting by the steersman, sunk in deep thought, but when he noticed in the water the reflection of these darting and wavering sparks and flames, he felt as if it were the little golden snakes that were sporting in the flood.   All the wonders that he had seen at the elder-tree again started forth into his heart and thoughts; and again that unspeakable longing, that glowing desire, laid hold of him here, which had agitated his bosom before in painful spasms of rapture.

"Ah! is it you again, my little golden snakes?   Sing now, O sing! In your song let the kind, dear, dark-blue eyes again appear to me—Ah! are you under the waves, then?"

So cried the Student Anselmus, and at the same time made a violent movement, as if he was about to plunge into the river.

"Is the Devil in you, sir?" exclaimed the steersman, and clutched him by the lapels. The girls, who were sitting by him, shrieked in terror, and fled to the other side of the gondola. Registrator Heerbrand whispered something in Conrector Paulmann's ear, to which the latter answered at considerable length, but in so low a tone that Anselmus could distinguish nothing but the words: "Such attacks more than once?—Never heard of it." Directly after this, Conrector Paulmann also rose, and then sat down, with a certain earnest, grave, official mien beside the Student Anselmus, taking his hand and saying: "How are you, Herr Anselmus?"

The Student Anselmus was almost losing his wits, for in his mind there was a mad contradiction, which he strove in vain to reconcile. He now saw plainly that what he had taken for the gleaming of the golden snakes was nothing but the reflection of the fireworks in Anton's Garden: but a feeling unexperienced till now, he himself did not know whether it was rapture or pain, cramped his breast together; and when the steersman struck through the water with his helm, so that the waves, curling as in anger, gurgled and chafed, he heard in their din a soft whispering: "Anselmus! Anselmus! do you see how we still skim along before you? Sisterkin looks at you again: believe, believe, believe in us!" And he thought he saw in the reflected light three green-glowing streaks: but then, when he gazed, full of fond sadness, into the water, to see whether those gentle eyes would not look up to him again, he perceived too well that the shine proceeded only from the windows in the neighbouring houses. He was sitting mute in his place, and inwardly battling with himself, when Conrector Paulmann repeated, with still greater emphasis: "How are you, Herr Anselmus?"

With the most rueful tone, Anselmus replied: "Ah! Herr Conrector, if you knew what strange things I have been dreaming, quite awake, with open eyes, just now, under an elder-tree at the wall of Linke's Garden, you would not take it amiss of me that I am a little absent, or so."

"Ey, ey, Herr Anselmus!" interrupted Conrector Paulmann, "I have always taken you for a solid young man: but to dream, to dream with your eyes wide open, and then, all at once, to start up and try to jump into the water! This, begging your pardon, is what only fools or madmen would do."

The Student Anselmus was deeply affected by his friend's hard saying; then Veronica, Paulmann's eldest daughter, a most pretty blooming girl of sixteen, addressed her father: "But, dear father, something singular must have befallen Herr Anselmus; and perhaps he only thinks he was awake, while he may have really been asleep, and so all manner of wild stuff has come into his head, and is still lying in his thoughts."

"And, dearest Mademoiselle! Worthy Conrector!" cried Registrator Heerbrand, "may one not, even when awake, sometimes sink into a sort of dream state? I myself have had such fits. One afternoon, for instance, during coffee, in a sort of brown study like this, in the special season of corporeal and spiritual digestion, the place where a lost *Act* was lying occurred to me, as if by inspiration; and last night, no farther gone, there came a glorious large Latin paper tripping out before my open eyes, in the very same way."

"Ah! most honoured Registrator," answered Conrector Paulmann, "you have always had a tendency to the *Poetica*; and thus one falls into fantasies and romantic humours."

The Student Anselmus, however, was particularly gratified that in this most troublous situation, while in danger of being considered drunk or crazy, anyone should take his part; and though it was already pretty dark, he thought he noticed, for the first time, that Veronica had really very fine dark blue eyes, and this too without remembering the strange pair which he had looked at in the elder-bush. Actually, the adventure under the elder-bush had once more entirely vanished from the thoughts of the Student Anselmus; he felt himself at ease and light of heart; nay, in the capriciousness of joy, he carried it so far, that he offered a helping hand to his fair advocate Veronica, as she was stepping from the gondola; and without more ado, as she put her arm in his, escorted her home with so much dexterity and good luck that he only missed his footing once, and this being the only wet spot in the whole road, only spattered Veronica's white gown a very little by the incident.

Conrector Paulmann did not fail to observe this happy change in the Student Anselmus; he resumed his liking for him and begged forgiveness for the hard words which he had let fall before. "Yes," added he, "we have many examples to show that certain phantasms may rise before a man, and pester and plague him not a little; but this is bodily disease, and leeches are good for it, if applied to the right part, as a certain learned physician, now deceased, has directed." The Student Anselmus did not know whether he had been drunk, crazy, or sick; but in any case the leeches seemed entirely superfluous, as these supposed phantasms had utterly vanished, and the Student himself was growing happier and happier the more he prospered in serving the pretty Veronica with all sorts of dainty attentions.

As usual, after the frugal meal, there came music; the Student Anselmus had to take his seat before the harpsichord, and Veronica accompanied his playing with her pure clear voice: "Dear Mademoiselle," said Registrator Heerbrand, "you have a voice like a crystal bell!"

"That she has not!" ejaculated the Student Anselmus, he scarcely knew how. "Crystal bells in elder-trees sound strangely! strangely!" continued the Student Anselmus, murmuring half aloud.

Veronica laid her hand on his shoulder, and asked: "What are you saying now, Herr Anselmus?"

Instantly Anselmus recovered his cheerfulness, and began playing. Conrector Paulmann gave him a grim look; but Registrator Heerbrand laid a music leaf on the rack, and sang with ravishing grace one of Bandmaster Graun's bravura airs. The Student Anselmus accompanied this, and much more; and a fantasy duet, which Veronica and he now fingered, and Conrector Paulmann had himself composed, again brought everyone into the gayest humour.

It was now pretty late, and Registrator Heerbrand was taking up his hat and stick, when Conrector Paulmann went up to him with a mysterious air, and said: "Hem!—Would not you, honoured Registrator, mention to the good Herr Anselmus himself—Hem! what we were speaking of before?"

"With all the pleasure in the world," said Registrator Heerbrand, and having placed himself in the circle, began, without farther preamble, as follows:

"In this city is a strange remarkable man; people say he follows all manner of secret sciences. But as there are no such sciences, I take him rather for an antiquary, and along with this for an experimental chemist. I mean no other than our Privy Archivarius Lindhorst. He lives, as you know, by himself, in his old isolated house; and when he is away from his office, he is to be found in his library or in his chemical laboratory, to which, however, he admits no stranger. Besides many curious books, he possesses a number of manuscripts, partly Arabic, Coptic, and some of them in strange characters, which do not belong to any known tongue. These he wishes to have copied properly, and for this purpose he requires a man who can draw with the pen, and so transfer these marks to parchment, in Indian ink, with the highest exactness and fidelity. The work is to be carried on in a separate chamber of his house, under his own supervision; and besides free board during the time of business, he will pay his copyist a speziesthaler, or specie-dollar, daily, and promises a handsome present when the copying is rightly finished. The hours of work are from twelve to six. From three to four, you take rest and dinner.

"Herr Archivarius Lindhorst having in vain tried one or two young people for copying these manuscripts, has at last applied to me to find him an expert calligrapher, and so I have been thinking of you, my dear Anselmus, for I know that you both write very neatly and draw with the pen to great perfection. Now, if in these bad times, and till your future establishment, you would like to earn a speziesthaler every day, and a present over and above your salary, you can go tomorrow precisely at noon, and call upon the Archivarius, whose house no doubt you know. But be on your guard against blots! If such a thing falls on your copy, you must begin it again; if it falls on the original, the Archivarius will think nothing of throwing you out the window, for he is a hot-tempered man."

The Student Anselmus was filled with joy at Registrator Heerbrand's proposal; for not only could the Student write well and draw well with the pen, but this copying with laborious calligraphic pains was a thing he delighted in more than anything else. So he thanked his patron in the most grateful terms, and promised not to fail at noon tomorrow.

All night the Student Anselmus saw nothing but clear speziesthalers, and heard nothing but their lovely clink. Who could blame the poor youth, cheated of so many hopes by capricious destiny, obliged to take counsel about every farthing, and to forego so many joys which a young heart requires! Early in the morning he brought out his black-lead pencils, his crowquills, his Indian ink; for better materials, thought he, the Archivarius can find nowhere. Above all, he gathered together and arranged his calligraphic masterpieces and his drawings, to show them to the Archivarius, as proof of his ability to do what was desired. Everything went well with the Student; a peculiar happy star seemed to be presiding over him; his neckcloth sat right at the very first trial; no stitches burst; no loop gave way in his black silk stockings; his hat did not once fall to the dust after he had trimmed it. In a word, precisely at half-past eleven, the Student Anselmus, in his pike-gray frock and black satin lower habiliments, with a roll of calligraphic specimens and pen-drawings in his pocket, was standing in the Schlossgasse, or Castle Alley, in Conradi's shop, and drinking one—two glasses of the best stomachic liqueur; for here, thought he, slapping his pocket, which was still empty, for here speziesthalers will soon be chinking.

Notwithstanding the distance of the solitary street where the
Archivarius Lindhorst's ancient residence lay, the Student Anselmus
was at the front door before the stroke of twelve. He stood there,
and was looking at the large fine bronze knocker; but now when, as
the last stroke tingled through the air with a loud clang from the
steeple clock of the Kreuzkirche, or Church of the Cross, he lifted
his hand to grasp this same knocker, the metal visage twisted itself,
with a horrid rolling of its blue-gleaming eyes, into a grinning smile.
Alas, it was the Applewoman of the Schwarzthor! The pointed
teeth gnashed together in the loose jaws, and in their chattering
through the skinny lips, there was a growl as of "You fool, fool,
fool!—Wait, wait!—Why did you run!—Fool!" Horror-struck,
the Student Anselmus flew back; he clutched at the door-post, but
his hand caught the bell-rope, and pulled it, and in piercing discords it rang stronger and stronger, and through the whole empty
house the echo repeated, as in mockery: "To the crystal, fall!"
An unearthly terror seized the Student Anselmus, and quivered
through all his limbs. The bell-rope lengthened downwards, and
became a gigantic, transparent, white serpent, which encircled and
crushed him, and girded him straiter and straiter in its coils, till his
brittle paralyzed limbs went crashing in pieces and the blood
spouted from his veins, penetrating into the transparent body of the
serpent and dyeing it red. "Kill me! Kill me!" he wanted to cry,
in his horrible agony; but the cry was only a stifled gurgle in his
throat. The serpent lifted its head, and laid its long peaked tongue
of glowing brass on the breast of Anselmus; then a fierce pang
suddenly cut asunder the artery of life, and thought fled away from
him. On returning to his senses, he was lying on his own poor
truckle-bed; Conrector Paulmann was standing before him, and
saying: "For Heaven's sake, what mad stuff is this, dear Herr
Anselmus?"

THIRD VIGIL

"The Spirit looked upon the water, and the water moved itself,
and chafed in foaming billows, and plunged thundering down into
the abysses, which opened their black throats and greedily swallowed
it. Like triumphant conquerors, the granite rocks lifted their cleft
peaky crowns, protecting the valley, till the sun took it into his
paternal bosom, and clasping it with his beams as with glowing
arms, cherished it and warmed it. Then a thousand germs, which

had been sleeping under the desert sand, awoke from their deep slumber, and stretched out their little leaves and stalks towards the sun their father's face; and like smiling infants in green cradles, the flowrets rested in their buds and blossoms, till they too, awakened by their father, decked themselves in lights, which their father, to please them, tinted in a thousand varied hues.

"But in the midst of the valley was a black hill, which heaved up and down like the breast of man when warm longing swells it. From the abysses mounted steaming vapours, which rolled themselves together into huge masses, striving malignantly to hide the father's face: but he called the storm to him, which rushed there, and scattered them away; and when the pure sunbeam rested again on the bleak hill, there started from it, in the excess of its rapture, a glorious Fire-lily, opening its fair leaves like gentle lips to receive the kiss of its father.

"And now came a gleaming splendour into the valley; it was the youth Phosphorus; the Lily saw him, and begged, being seized with warm longing love: 'Be mine for ever, fair youth! For I love you, and must die if you forsake me!' Then spoke the youth Phosphorus: 'I will be yours, fair flower; but then, like a naughty child, you will leave father and mother; you will know your playmates no longer, will strive to be greater and stronger than all that now rejoices with you as your equal. The longing which now beneficently warms your whole being will be scattered into a thousand rays and torture and vex you, for sense will bring forth senses; and the highest rapture, which the spark I cast into you kindles, will be the hopeless pain wherein you shall perish, to spring up anew in foreign shape. This spark is thought!'

"'Ah!' mourned the Lily, 'can I not be yours in this glow, as it now burns in me; not still be yours? Can I love you more than now; could I look on you as now, if you were to annihilate me?' Then the youth Phosphorus kissed the Lily; and as if penetrated with light, it mounted up in flame, out of which issued a foreign being, that hastily flying from the valley, roved forth into endless space, no longer heeding its old playmates, or the youth it had loved. This youth mourned for his lost beloved; for he too loved her, it was love to the fair Lily that had brought him to the lone valley; and the granite rocks bent down their heads in participation of his grief.

"But one of these opened its bosom, and there came a black-winged dragon flying out of it, who said: 'My brethren, the Metals are sleeping in there; but I am always brisk and waking, and will help you.' Dashing forth on its black pinions, the dragon at last caught **the be**ing which had sprung from the Lily; bore it to the hill, and encircled it with his wing; then was it the Lily again; but thought, which continued with it, tore asunder its heart; and its love for the youth Phosphorus was a cutting pain, before which, as if breathed on by poisonous vapours, the flowrets which had once rejoiced in the fair Lily's presence, faded and died.

"The youth Phosphorus put on a glittering coat of mail, sporting with the light in a thousand hues, and did battle with the dragon, who struck the cuirass with his black wing, till it rung and sounded; and at this loud clang the flowrets again came to life, and like variegated birds fluttered round the dragon, whose force departed; and who, thus being vanquished, hid himself in the depths of the earth. The Lily was freed; the youth Phosphorus clasped her, full of warm longing, of heavenly love; and in triumphant chorus, the flowers, the birds, nay, even the high granite rocks, did reverence to her as the Queen of the Valley."

"By your leave, worthy Herr Archivarius, this is Oriental bombast," said Registrator Heerbrand: "and we beg very much you would rather, as you often do, give us something of your own most remarkable life, of your travelling adventures, for instance; above all, something true."

"What the deuce, then?" answered Archivarius Lindhorst. "True? This very thing I have been telling is the truest I could dish out for you, my friends, and belongs to my life too, in a certain sense. For I come from that very valley; and the Fire-lily, which at last ruled as queen there, was my great-great-great-great-grandmother; and so, properly speaking, I am a prince myself." All burst into a peal of laughter. "Ay, laugh your fill," continued Archivarius Lindhorst. "To you this matter, which I have related, certainly in the most brief and meagre way, may seem senseless and mad; yet, notwithstanding this, it is meant for anything but incoherent, or even allegorical, and it is, in one word, literally true. Had I known, however, that the glorious love story, to which I owe my existence, would have pleased you so little, I might have given you a little of the news my brother brought me on his visit yesterday."

"What, what is this? Have you a brother, then, Herr Archivarius? Where is he? Where does he live? In his Majesty's service too? Or perhaps a private scholar?" cried the company from all quarters.

"No!" replied the Archivarius, quite cool, composedly taking a pinch of snuff, "he has joined the bad side; he has gone over to the Dragons."

"What do you mean, dear Herr Archivarius?" cried Registrator Heerbrand: "Over to the Dragons?"—"Over to the Dragons?" resounded like an echo from all hands.

"Yes, over to the Dragons," continued Archivarius Lindhorst: "it was sheer desperation, I believe. You know, gentlemen, my father died a short while ago; it is but three hundred and eighty-five years ago at most, and I am still in mourning for it. He had left me, his favourite son, a fine onyx; this onyx, rightly or wrongly, my brother would have: we quarrelled about it, over my father's corpse; in such unseemly manner that the good man started up, out of all patience, and threw my wicked brother downstairs. This stuck in our brother's stomach, and so without loss of time he went over to the Dragons. At present, he lives in a cypress wood, not far from Tunis: he has a famous magical carbuncle to watch there, which a dog of necromancer, who has set up a summerhouse in Lapland, has an eye to; so my poor brother only gets away for a quarter of an hour or so, when the necromancer happens to be out looking after the salamander bed in his garden, and then he tells me in all haste what good news there is about the Springs of the Nile."

For the second time, the company burst out into a peal of laughter: but the Student Anselmus began to feel quite dreary in heart; and he could scarcely look in Archivarius Lindhorst's parched countenance, and fixed earnest eyes, without shuddering internally in a way which he could not himself understand. Moreover, in the harsh and strangely metallic sound of Archivarius Lindhorst's voice there was something mysteriously piercing for the Student Anselmus, and he felt his very bones and marrow tingling as the Archivarius spoke.

The special object for which Registrator Heerbrand had taken him into the coffee house, seemed at present not attainable. After that accident at Archivarius Lindhorst's door, the Student Anselmus had withstood all inducements to risk a second visit: for, according to his own heart-felt conviction, it was only chance that had saved him, if not from death, at least from the danger of insanity. Conrector Paulmann had happened to be passing through the street at the time when Anselmus was lying quite senseless at the door, and an old woman, who had laid her cookie-and-apple basket aside, was busied about him. Conrector Paulmann had forthwith called a chair, and so had him carried home. "Think what you will of me," said the Student Anselmus, "consider me a fool or not: I say, the cursed visage of that witch at the Schwarzthor grinned on me from the doorknocker. What happened after I would rather not speak of: but if I had recovered from my faint and seen that infernal Apple-wife beside me (for the old woman whom you talk of was no other), I should that instant have been struck by apoplexy, or have run stark mad."

All persuasions, all sensible arguments on the part of Conrector Paulmann and Registrator Heerbrand, profited nothing; and even the blue-eyed Veronica herself could not raise him from a certain moody humour, in which he had ever since been sunk. In fact, these friends regarded him as troubled in mind, and considered ways for diverting his thoughts; to which end, Registrator Heerbrand thought, there could nothing be so serviceable as copying Archivarius Lindhorst's manuscripts. The business, therefore, was to introduce the Student in some proper way to Archivarius Lindhorst; and so Registrator Heerbrand, knowing that the Archivarius used to visit a certain coffee house almost nightly, had invited the Student Anselmus to come every evening to that same coffee house, and drink a glass of beer and smoke a pipe, at his, the Registrator's charge, till such time as Archivarius Lindhorst should in one way or another see him, and the bargain for this copying work be settled; which offer the Student Anselmus had most gratefully accepted. "God will reward you, worthy Registrator, if you bring the young man to reason!" said Conrector Paulmann. "God will reward you!" repeated Veronica, piously raising her eyes to heaven, and vividly thinking that the Student Anselmus was already a most pretty young man, even without any reason.

Now accordingly, as Archivarius Lindhorst, with hat and staff, was making for the door, Registrator Heerbrand seized the Student Anselmus briskly by the hand, and stepping to meet the Herr Archivarius, he said: "Most esteemed Herr Archivarius, here is the Student Anselmus, who has an uncommon talent in calligraphy and drawing, and will undertake the copying of your rare manuscripts."

"I am most particularly glad to hear it," answered Archivarius Lindhorst sharply, then threw his three-cocked military hat on his head, and shoving Registrator Heerbrand and the Student Anselmus aside, rushed downstairs with great tumult, so that both of them were left standing in great confusion, gaping at the door, which he had slammed in their faces till the bolts and hinges of it rung again.

"He is a very strange old gentleman," said Registrator Heerbrand. "Strange old gentleman," stammered the Student Anselmus, with a feeling as if an ice-stream were creeping over all his veins, and he were stiffening into a statue. All the guests, however, laughed, and said: "Our Archivarius is on his high horse today: tomorrow, you shall see, he will be mild as a lamb again, and won't speak a word, but will look into the smoke-vortexes of his pipe, or read the newspapers; you must not mind these freaks."

"That is true too," thought the Student Anselmus: "who would mind such a thing, after all? Did not the Archivarius tell me he was most particularly glad to hear that I would undertake the copying of his manuscripts; and why did Registrator Heerbrand step directly in his way, when he was going home? No, no, he is a good man at bottom this Privy Archivarius Lindhorst, and surprisingly liberal. A little curious in his figures of speech; but what is that to me? Tomorrow at the stroke of twelve I will go to him, though fifty bronze Apple-wives should try to hinder me!"

FOURTH VIGIL

Gracious reader, may I venture to ask you a question? Have you ever had hours, perhaps even days or weeks, in which all your customary activities did nothing but cause you vexation and dissatisfaction; when everything that you usually consider worthy and important seemed trivial and worthless? At such a time you did not know what to do or where to turn. A dim feeling pervaded your breast that you had higher desires that must be fulfilled, desires that transcended the pleasures of this world, yet desires which your spirit, like a cowed child, did not even dare to utter. In this longing for an unknown Something, which longing hovered above you no matter where you were, like an airy dream with thin transparent forms that melted away each time you tried to examine them, you had no voice for the world about you. You passed to and fro with troubled look, like a hopeless lover, and no matter what you saw being attempted or attained in the bustle of varied existence, it awakened no sorrow or joy in you. It was as if you had no share in this sublunary world.

If, favourable reader, you have ever been in this mood, you know the state into which the Student Anselmus had fallen. I wish most heartily, courteous reader, that it were in my power to bring the Student Anselmus before your eyes with true vividness. For in these vigils in which I record his singular history, there is still so much more of the marvellous—which is likely to make the everyday life of ordinary mortals seem pallid—that I fear in the end you will believe in neither the Student Anselmus nor Archivarius Lindhorst; indeed, that you will even entertain doubts as to Registrator

Heerbrand and Conrector Paulmann, though these two estimable persons, at least, are still walking the pavements of Dresden. Favourable reader, while you are in the faery region of glorious wonders, where both rapture and horror may be evoked; where the goddess of earnestness herself will waft her veil aside and show her countenance (though a smile often glimmers in her glance, a sportive teasing before perplexing enchantments, comparable to mothers nursing and dandling their children)—while you are in this region which the spirit lays open to us in dreams, make an effort to recognize the well-known forms which hover around you in fitful brightness even in ordinary life. You will then find that this glorious kingdom lies much closer at hand than you ever supposed; it is this kingdom which I now very heartily desire, and am striving to show you in the singular story of the Student Anselmus.

So, as was hinted, the Student Anselmus, ever since that evening when he met with Archivarius Lindhorst, had been sunk in a dreamy musing, which rendered him insensible to every outward touch from common life. He felt that an unknown Something was awakening his inmost soul, and calling forth that rapturous pain, which is even the mood of longing that announces a loftier existence to man. He delighted most when he could rove alone through meads and woods; and as if released from all that fettered him to his necessary life, could, so to speak, again find himself in the manifold images which mounted from his soul.

It happened once that in returning from a long ramble, he passed by that notable elder-tree, under which, as if taken with faery, he had formerly beheld so many marvels. He felt himself strangely attracted by the green kindly sward; but no sooner had he seated himself on it than the whole vision which he had previously seen as in a heavenly trance, and which had since as if by foreign influence been driven from his mind, again came floating before him in the liveliest colours, as if he had been looking on it a second time. Nay, it was clearer to him now than ever, that the gentle blue eyes belonged to the gold-green snake, which had wound itself through the middle of the elder-tree; and that from the turnings of its tapering body all those glorious crystal tones, which had filled him with rapture, must have broken forth. As on Ascension Day, he again clasped the elder-tree to his bosom, and cried into the twigs and leaves: "Ah, once more shoot forth, and turn and wind yourself among the twigs, little fair green snake, that I may see you! Once more look at me with your gentle eyes! Ah, I love you, and must die in pain and grief, if you do not return!" All, however, remained quite dumb and still; and as before, the elder-tree rustled quite unintelligibly with its twigs and leaves. But the Student Anselmus now felt as if he knew what it was that so moved and worked within him, nay, that so tore his bosom in the pain of an infinite longing. "What else is it," said he, "but that I love you with my whole heart and soul, and even to the death, glorious little golden snake; nay, that without you I cannot live, and must perish in hopeless woe, unless I find you again, unless I have you as the beloved of my heart. But I know it, you shall be mine; and then all that glorious dreams have promised me of another higher world shall be fulfilled."

Henceforth the Student Anselmus, every evening, when the sun was scattering its bright gold over the peaks of the trees, was to be seen under the elder-bush, calling from the depths of his heart in most lamentable tones into the branches and leaves for a sight of his beloved, of his little gold-green snake. Once as he was going on with this, there suddenly stood before him a tall lean man, wrapped up in a wide light-gray surtout, who, looking at him with large fiery eyes, exclaimed: "Hey, hey, what whining and whimpering is this? Hey, hey, this is Herr Anselmus that was to copy my manu-scripts." The Student Anselmus felt not a little terrified at hearing this voice, for it was the very same which on Ascension Day had called: "Hey, hey, what chattering and jingling is this," and so forth. For fright and astonishment, he could not utter a word. "What ails you, Herr Anselmus," continued Archivarius Lindhorst, for the stranger was no one else; "what do you want with the elder-tree, and why did you not come to me and set about your work?"

In fact, the Student Anselmus had never yet prevailed upon himself to visit Archivarius Lindhorst's house a second time, though, that evening, he had firmly resolved on doing it. But now at this moment, when he saw his fair dreams torn asunder, and that too by the same hostile voice which had once before snatched away his beloved, a sort of desperation came over him, and he broke out fiercely into these words: "You may think me mad or not, Herr Archivarius; it is all the same to me: but here in this bush, on Ascension Day, I saw the gold-green snake—ah! the beloved of my soul; and she spoke to me in glorious crystal tones; and you, you, Herr Archivarius, cried and shouted horribly over the water."

"How is this, my dear sir?" interrupted Archivarius Lindhorst, smiling quite inexpressibly, and taking snuff.

The Student Anselmus felt his breast becoming easy, now that he had succeeded in beginning this strange story; and it seemed to him as if he were quite right in laying the whole blame upon the Archivarius, and that it was he, and no one else, who had thundered so from the distance. He courageously proceeded: "Well, then, I will tell you the whole mystery that happened to me on Ascension evening; and then you may say and do, and think of me whatever you please." He accordingly disclosed the whole miraculous adventure, from his luckless upsetting of the apple basket, till the departure of the three gold-green snakes over the river; and how the people after that had thought him drunk or crazy. "All this," ended the Student Anselmus, "I actually saw with my eyes; and deep in my bosom those dear voices, which spoke to me, are still sounding in clear echo: it was in no way a dream; and if I am not to die of longing and desire, I must believe in these gold-green snakes, though I see by your smile, Herr Archivarius, that you hold these same snakes as nothing more than creatures of my heated and overstrained imagination."

"Not at all," replied the Archivarius, with the greatest calmness and composure; "the gold-green snakes, which you saw in the elder-bush, Herr Anselmus, were simply my three daughters; and that you have fallen over head and ears in love with the blue eyes of Serpentina the youngest, is now clear enough. Indeed, I knew it on Ascension Day myself: and as (on that occasion, sitting busied with my writing at home) I began to get annoyed with so much chattering and jingling, I called to the idle minxes that it was time to get home, for the sun was setting, and they had sung and basked enough."

The Student Anselmus felt as if he now merely heard in plain words something he had long dreamed of, and though he fancied he observed that elder-bush, wall and sward, and all objects about him were beginning slowly to whirl around, he took heart, and was ready to speak; but the Archivarius prevented him; for sharply pulling the glove from his left hand, and holding the stone of a ring, glittering in strange sparkles and flames before the Student's eyes, he said: "Look here, Herr Anselmus; what you see may do you good."

The Student Anselmus looked in, and O wonder! the stone emitted a cluster of rays; and the rays wove themselves together into a clear gleaming crystal mirror; in which, with many windings, now flying asunder, now twisted together, the three gold-green snakes were dancing and bounding. And when their tapering forms, glittering with a thousand sparkles, touched each other, there issued from them glorious tones, as of crystal bells; and the midmost of the three stretched forth her little head from the mirror, as if full of longing and desire, and her dark-blue eyes said: "Do you know me, then? Do you believe in me, Anselmus? In belief alone is love: can you love?"

"O Serpentina! Serpentina!" cried the Student Anselmus in mad rapture; but Archivarius Lindhorst suddenly breathed on the mirror, and with an electric sputter the rays sank back into their focus; and on his hand there was now nothing but a little emerald, over which the Archivarius drew his glove.

"Did you see the golden snakes, Herr Anselmus?" said the Archivarius.

"Ah, good heaven, yes!" replied the Student, "and the fair dear Serpentina."

"Hush!" continued Archivarius Lindhorst, "enough for now: for the rest, if you decide to work with me, you may see my daughter often enough; or rather I will grant you this real satisfaction: if you stick tightly and truly to your task, that is to say, copy every mark with the greatest clearness and correctness. But you have not come to me at all, Herr Anselmus, although Registrator Heerbrand promised I should see you immediately, and I have waited several days in vain."

Not until the mention of Registrator Heerbrand's name did the Student Anselmus again feel as if he was really standing with his two legs on the ground, and he was really the Student Anselmus, and the man talking to him really Archivarius Lindhorst. The tone of indifference, with which the latter spoke, in such rude contrast with the strange sights which like a genuine necromancer he had called forth, awakened a certain horror in the Student, which the piercing look of those fiery eyes, glowing from their bony sockets in the lean puckered visage, as from a leathern case, still farther aggravated: and the Student was again forcibly seized with the same unearthly feeling, which had before gained possession of him in the coffee house, when Archivarius Lindhorst had talked so wildly. With a great effort he retained his self-command, and as the Archivarius again asked, "Well, why did you not come?" the Student exerted his whole energies, and related to him what had happened at the street door.

"My dear Herr Anselmus," said the Archivarius, when the Student was finished; "dear Herr Anselmus, I know this Apple-wife of whom you speak; she is a vicious slut that plays all sorts of vile tricks on me; but that she has turned herself to bronze and taken the shape of a doorknocker, to deter pleasant visitors from calling, is indeed very bad, and truly not to be endured. Would you please, worthy Herr Anselmus, if you come tomorrow at noon and notice any more of this grinning and growling, just be so good as to let a drop or two of this liquor fall on her nose; it will put everything to rights immediately. And now, adieu, my dear Herr Anselmus! I must make haste, therefore I would not advise you to think of returning with me. Adieu, till we meet!—Tomorrow at noon!"

The Archivarius had given the Student Anselmus a little vial, with a gold-coloured fluid in it; and he walked rapidly off; so rapidly, that in the dusk, which had now come on, he seemed to be floating down to the valley rather than walking down to it. Already he was near the Kosel garden; the wind got within his wide greatcoat, and drove its breasts asunder; so that they fluttered in the air like a pair of large wings; and to the Student Anselmus, who was looking full of amazement at the course of the Archivarius, it seemed as if a large bird were spreading out its pinions for rapid flight. And now, while the Student kept gazing into the dusk, a white-gray kite with creaking cry soared up into the air; and he now saw clearly that the white flutter which he had thought to be the retiring Archivarius must have been this very kite, though he still could not understand where the Archivarius had vanished so abruptly.

"Perhaps he may have flown away in person, this Herr Archivarius Lindhorst," said the Student Anselmus to himself; "for I now see and feel clearly, that all these foreign shapes of a distant wondrous world, which I never saw before except in peculiarly remarkable dreams, have now come into my waking life, and are making their sport of me. But be this as it will! You live and glow in my breast, lovely, gentle Serpentina; you alone can still the infinite longing which rends my soul to pieces. Ah, when shall I see your kind eyes, dear, dear Serpentina!" cried the Student Anselmus aloud.

"That is a vile unchristian name!" murmured a bass voice beside him, which belonged to some promenader returning home. The Student Anselmus, reminded where he was, hastened off at a quick pace, thinking to himself: "Wouldn't it be a real misfortune now if Conrector Paulmann or Registrator Heerbrand were to meet me?"—But neither of these gentlemen met him.

FIFTH VIGIL

"There is nothing in the world that can be done with this Anselmus," said Conrector Paulmann; "all my good advice, all my admonitions, are fruitless; he will apply himself to nothing; though he is a fine classical scholar too, and that is the foundation of everything."

But Registrator Heerbrand, with a sly, mysterious smile, replied: "Let Anselmus take his time, my dear Conrector! he is a strange subject, this Anselmus, but there is much in him: and when I say much, I mean a Privy Secretary, or even a Court Councillor, a Hofrath."

"Hof——" began Conrector Paulmann, in the deepest amazement; the word stuck in his throat.

"Hush! hush!" continued Registrator Heerbrand, "I know what I know. These two days he has been with Archivarius Lindhorst, copying manuscripts; and last night the Archivarius meets me at the coffee house, and says: 'You have sent me a proper man, good neighbour! There is stuff in him!' And now think of Archivarius Lindhorst's influence—Hush! hush! we will talk of it this time a year from now." And with these words the Registrator, his face still wrinkled into the same sly smile, went out of the room, leaving the Conrector speechless with astonishment and curiosity, and fixed, as if by enchantment, in his chair.

But on Veronica this dialogue had made a still deeper impression. "Did I not know all along," she thought, "that Herr Anselmus was a most clever and pretty young man, to whom something great would come? Were I but certain that he really liked me! But that night when we crossed the Elbe, did he not press my hand twice? Did he not look at me, in our duet, with such glances that pierced into my very heart? Yes, yes! he really likes me; and I ——" Veronica gave herself up, as young maidens are wont, to sweet dreams of a gay future. She was Mrs. Hofrath, Frau Hofräthinn; she occupied a fine house in the Schlossgasse, or in the Neumarkt, or in the Moritzstrasse; her fashionable hat, her new Turkish shawl, became her admirably; she was breakfasting on the balcony in an elegant negligée, giving orders to her cook for the day: "And see, if you please, not to spoil that dish; it is the Hofrath's favourite." Then passing beaux glanced up, and she heard distinctly: "Well, she is a heavenly woman, that Hofräthinn; how prettily the lace cap suits her!" Mrs. Privy Councillor Ypsilon sends her servant to ask if it would please the Frau Hofräthinn to drive as far as the Linke Bath today? "Many compliments; extremely sorry, I am engaged to tea already with the Presidentinn Tz." Then comes the Hofrath Anselmus back from his office; he is dressed in the top of the mode: "Ten, I declare," cries he, making his gold watch repeat, and giving his young lady a kiss. "How are things, little wife? Guess what I have here for you?" he continues in a teasing manner, and draws from his waistcoat pocket a pair of beautiful earrings, fashioned in the newest style, and puts them on in place of the old ones. "Ah! What pretty, dainty earrings!" cried Veronica aloud; and started up from her chair, throwing aside her work, to see those fair earrings with her own eyes in the glass.

"What is this?" said Conrector Paulmann, roused by the noise from his deep study of *Cicero de Officiis*, and almost dropping the book from his hand; "are we taking fits, like Anselmus?" But at this moment, the Student Anselmus, who, contrary to his custom, had not been seen for several days, entered the room, to Veronica's astonishment and terror; for, in truth, he seemed altered in his whole bearing. With a certain precision, which was far from usual in him, he spoke of new tendencies of life which had become clear to his mind, of glorious prospects which were opening for him, but which many did not have the skill to discern. Conrector Paulmann, remembering Registrator Heerbrand's mysterious speech, was still more struck, and could scarcely utter a syllable, till the Student Anselmus, after letting fall some hints of urgent business at Archivarius Lindhorst's, and with elegant adroitness kissing Veronica's hand, was already down the stairs, off and away.

"This was the Hofrath," murmured Veronica to herself: "and he kissed my hand, without sliding on the floor, or treading on my foot, as he used to! He threw me the softest look too; yes, he really loves me!"

Veronica again gave way to her dreaming; yet now, it was as if a hostile shape were still coming forward among these lovely visions of her future household life as Frau Hofräthinn, and the shape were laughing in spiteful mockery, and saying: "This is all very stupid and trashy stuff, and lies to boot; for Anselmus will never, never, be Hofrath or your husband; he does not love you in the least, though you have blue eyes, and a fine figure, and a pretty hand." Then an ice-stream poured over Veronica's soul; and a deep sorrow swept away the delight with which, a little while ago, she had seen herself in the lace cap and fashionable earrings. Tears almost rushed into her eyes, and she said aloud: "Ah! it is too true; he does not love me in the least; and I shall never, never, be Frau Hofräthinn!"

"Romantic idiocy, romantic idiocy!" cried Conrector Paulmann; then snatched his hat and stick, and hastened indignantly from the house. "This was still wanting," sighed Veronica; and felt vexed at her little sister, a girl of twelve years, because she sat so unconcerned, and kept sewing at her frame, as if nothing had happened.

Meanwhile it was almost three o'clock; and now time to tidy up the apartment, and arrange the coffee table: for the Mademoiselles Oster had announced that they were coming. But from behind every workbox which Veronica lifted aside, behind the notebooks which she took away from the harpsichord, behind every cup, behind the coffeepot which she took from the cupboard, that shape peeped forth, like a little mandrake, and laughed in spiteful mockery, and snapped its little spider fingers, and cried: "He will not be your husband! he will not be your husband!" And then, when she threw everything away, and fled to the middle of the room, it peered out again, with long nose, in gigantic bulk, from behind the stove, and snarled and growled: "He will not be your husband!"

"Don't you hear anything, don't you see anything?" cried Veronica, shivering with fright, and not daring to touch anything in the room. Fränzchen rose, quite grave and quiet, from her embroidering frame, and said, "What ails you today, sister? You are just making a mess. I must help you, I see."

But at this time the visitors came tripping in in a lively manner, with brisk laughter; and the same moment, Veronica perceived that it was the stove handle which she had taken for a shape, and the creaking of the ill-shut stove door for those spiteful words. Yet, overcome with horror, she did not immediately recover her composure, and her excitement, which her paleness and agitated looks betrayed, was noticed by the Mademoiselles Oster. As they at once cut short their merry talk, and pressed her to tell them what, in Heaven's name, had happened, Veronica was obliged to admit that certain strange thoughts had come into her mind; and suddenly, in open day a dread of spectres, which she did not normally feel, had got the better of her. She described in such lively colours how a little gray mannikin, peeping out of all the corners of the room, had mocked and plagued her, that the Mademoiselles Oster began to look around with timid glances, and began to have all sorts of unearthly notions. But Fränzchen entered at this moment with the steaming coffeepot; and the three, taking thought again, laughed outright at their folly.

Angelica, the elder of the Osters, was engaged to an officer; the young man had joined the army; but his friends had been so long without news of him that there was too little doubt of his being dead, or at least grievously wounded. This had plunged Angelica into the deepest sorrow; but today she was merry, even to extravagance, a state of things which so much surprised Veronica that she could not but speak of it, and inquire the reason.

"Darling," said Angelica, "do you fancy that my Victor is out of heart and thoughts? It is because of him I am so happy. O Heaven! so happy, so blessed in my whole soul! For my Victor is well; in a little while he will be home, advanced to Rittmeister, and decorated with the honours which he has won. A deep but not dangerous wound, in his right arm, which he got from a sword cut by a French hussar, prevents him from writing; and rapid change of quarters, for he will not consent to leave his regiment, makes it impossible for him to send me tidings. But tonight he will be ordered home, until his wound is cured. Tomorrow he will set out for home; and just as he is stepping into the coach, he will learn of his promotion to Rittmeister."

"But, my dear Angelica," interrupted Veronica. "How do you know all this?"

"Do not laugh at me, my friend," continued Angelica; "and surely you will not laugh, for the little gray mannikin, to punish you, might peep out from behind the mirror there. I cannot lay aside my belief in certain mysterious things, since often enough in life they have come before my eyes, I might say, into my very hands. For example, I cannot consider it so strange and incredible as many others do, that there should be people gifted with a certain faculty of prophecy. In the city, here, is an old woman, who possesses this gift to a high degree. She does not use cards, nor molten lead, nor coffee grounds, like ordinary fortune tellers, but after certain preparations, in which you yourself take a part, she takes a polished metallic mirror, and the strangest mixture of figures and forms, all intermingled rise up in it. She interprets these and answers your question. I was with her last night, and got those tidings of my Victor, which I have not doubted for a moment."

Angelica's narrative threw a spark into Veronica's soul, which instantly kindled with the thought of consulting this same old prophetess about Anselmus and her hopes. She learned that the crone was called Frau Rauerin, and lived in a remote street near the Seethor; that she was not to be seen except on Tuesdays, Thursdays, and Fridays, from seven o'clock in the evening, but then, indeed, through the whole night till sunrise; and that she preferred her customers to come alone. It was now Thursday, and Veronica determined, under pretext of accompanying the Osters home, to visit this old woman, and lay the case before her.

Accordingly, no sooner had her friends, who lived in the Neustadt, parted from her at the Elbe Bridge, than she hastened towards the Seethor; and before long, she had reached the remote narrow street described to her, and at the end of it saw the little red house in which Frau Rauerin was said to live. She could not rid herself of a certain dread, nay, of a certain horror, as she approached the door. At last she summoned resolution, in spite of inward terror, and made bold to pull the bell: the door opened, and she groped through the dark passage for the stair which led to the upper story, as Angelica had directed. "Does Frau Rauerin live here?" cried she into the empty lobby as no one appeared; but instead of an answer, there rose a long clear "Mew!" and a large black cat, with its back curved up, and whisking its tail to and fro in wavy coils, stepped on before her, with much gravity, to the door of the apartment, which, on a second mew, was opened.

"Ah, see! Are you here already, daughter? Come in, love; come in!" exclaimed an advancing figure, whose appearance rooted Veronica to the floor. A long lean woman, wrapped in black rags!—while she spoke, her peaked projecting chin wagged this way and that; her toothless mouth, overshadowed by a bony hawk-nose, twisted itself into a ghastly smile, and gleaming cat's-eyes flickered in sparkles through the large spectacles. From a party-coloured clout wrapped round her head, black wiry hair was sticking out; but what deformed her haggard visage to absolute horror, were two large burn marks which ran from the left cheek, over the nose. Veronica's breathing stopped; and the scream, which was about to lighten her choked breast, became a deep sigh, as the witch's skeleton hand took hold of her, and led her into the chamber. Here everything was awake and astir; nothing but din and tumult, and squeaking, and mewing, and croaking, and piping all at once, on every hand. The crone struck the table with her fist, and screamed: "Peace, ye vermin!" And the meer-cats, whimpering, clambered to the top of the high bed; and the little meer-swine all ran beneath the stove, and the raven fluttered up to the round mirror; and the black cat, as if the rebuke did not apply to him, kept sitting at his ease on the cushioned chair, to which he had leapt directly after entering.

So soon as the room became quiet, Veronica took heart; she felt less frightened than she had outside in the hall; nay, the crone herself did not seem so hideous. For the first time, she now looked round the room. All sorts of odious stuffed beasts hung down from the ceiling: strange unknown household implements were lying in confusion on the floor; and in the grate was a scanty blue fire, which only now and then sputtered up in yellow sparkles; and at every sputter, there came a rustling from above and monstrous bats, as if with human countenances in distorted laughter, went flitting to and fro; at times, too, the flame shot up, licking the sooty wall, and then there sounded cutting howling tones of woe, which shook Veronica with fear and horror. "With your leave, Mamsell!" said the crone, knitting her brows, and seizing a brush; with which, having dipped it in a copper skillet, she then besprinkled the grate. The fire went out; and as if filled with thick smoke, the room grew pitch-dark: but the crone, who had gone aside into a closet, soon returned with a lighted lamp; and now Veronica could see no beasts or implements in the apartment; it was a common meanly furnished room. The crone came up to her, and said with a creaking voice: "I know what you wish, little daughter: tush, you would have me tell you whether you shall wed Anselmus, when he is Hofrath."

Veronica stiffened with amazement and terror, but the crone continued: "You told me the whole of it at home, at your father's, when the coffeepot was standing before you: I was the coffeepot; didn't you know me? Daughterkin, hear me! Give up, give up this Anselmus; he is a nasty creature; he trod my little sons to pieces, my dear little sons, the Apples with the red cheeks, that glide away, when people have bought them, whisk! out of their pockets, and roll back into my basket. He trades with the Old One: it was but the day before yesterday, he poured that cursed Auripigment on my face, and I nearly went blind with it. You can see the burn marks yet. Daughterkin, give him up, give him up! He does not love you, for he loves the gold-green snake; he will never be Hofrath, for he has joined the salamanders, and he means to wed the green snake: give him up, give him up!"

Veronica, who had a firm, steadfast spirit of her own, and could conquer girlish terror, now drew back a step, and said, with a serious resolute tone: "Old woman! I heard of your gift of looking into the future; and wished, perhaps too curiously and thoughtlessly, to learn from you whether Anselmus, whom I love and value, could ever be mine. But if, instead of fulfilling my desire, you keep vexing me with your foolish unreasonable babble, you are doing wrong; for I have asked of you nothing but what you grant to others, as I well know. Since you are acquainted with my inmost thoughts apparently, it might perhaps have been an easy matter for you to unfold to me much that now pains and grieves my mind;

but after your silly slander of the good Anselmus, I do not care to talk further with you.   Goodnight!"

Veronica started to leave hastily, but the crone, with tears and lamentation, fell upon her knees; and, holding the young lady by the gown, exclaimed: "Veronica!   Veronica! have you forgotten old Liese?   Your nurse who has so often carried you in her arms, and dandled you?"

Veronica could scarcely believe her eyes; for here, in truth, was her old nurse, defaced only by great age and by the two burns; old Liese, who had vanished from Conrector Paulmann's house some years ago, no one knew where.   The crone, too, had quite another look now: instead of the ugly many-pieced clout, she had on a decent cap; instead of the black rags, a gay printed bedgown; she was neatly dressed, as of old.   She rose from the floor, and taking Veronica in her arms, proceeded: "What I have just told you may seem very mad; but, unluckily, it is too true.   Anselmus has done me much mischief, though it is not his own fault: he has fallen into Archivarius Lindhorst's hands, and the Old One means to marry him to his daughter.   Archivarius Lindhorst is my deadliest enemy: I could tell you thousands of things about him, which, however, you would not understand, or at best be too much frightened at.   He is the Wise Man, it seems; but I am the Wise Woman: let this stand for that!   I see now that you love this Anselmus; and I will help you with all my strength, that so you may be happy, and wed him like a pretty bride, as you wish."

"But tell me, for Heaven's sake, Liese——" interrupted Veronica.

"Hush! child, hush!" cried the old woman, interrupting in her turn: "I know what you would say; I have become what I am, because it was to be so: I could do no other.   Well, then! I know the means which will cure Anselmus of his frantic love for the green snake, and lead him, the prettiest Hofrath, into your arms; but you yourself must help."

"Tell me, Liese; I will do anything and everything, for I love Anselmus very much!" whispered Veronica, scarcely audibly.

"I know you," continued the crone, "for a courageous child: I could never frighten you to sleep with the *Wauwau*; for that instant, your eyes were open to what the *Wauwau* was like.   You would go without a light into the darkest room; and many a time, with papa's powder-mantle, you terrified the neighbours' children.   Well, then, if you are in earnest about conquering Archivarius Lindhorst and the green snake by my art; if you are in earnest about calling Anselmus Hofrath and husband; then, at the next Equinox, about eleven at night, glide from your father's house, and come here: I will go with you to the crossroads, which cut the fields hard by here: we shall take what is needed, and whatever wonders you may see shall do you no whit of harm. And now, love, goodnight: Papa is waiting for you at supper."

Veronica hastened away: she had the firmest purpose not to neglect the night of the Equinox; "for," thought she, "old Liese is right; Anselmus has become entangled in strange fetters; but I will free him from them, and call him mine forever; mine he is, and shall be, the Hofrath Anselmus."

SIXTH VIGIL

"It may be, after all," said the Student Anselmus to himself, "that the superfine strong stomachic liqueur, which I took somewhat freely in Monsieur Conradi's, might really be the cause of all these shocking phantasms, which tortured me so at Archivarius Lindhorst's door. Therefore, I will go quite sober today, and so bid defiance to whatever farther mischief may assail me." On this occasion, as before when equipping himself for his first call on Archivarius Lindhorst, the Student Anselmus put his pen-drawings, and calligraphic masterpieces, his bars of Indian ink, and his well-pointed crow-pens, into his pockets; and was just turning to go out, when his eye lighted on the vial with the yellow liquor, which he had received from Archivarius Lindhorst. All the strange adventures he had met again rose on his mind in glowing colours; and a nameless emotion of rapture and pain thrilled through his breast. Involuntarily he exclaimed, with a most piteous voice: "Ah, am not I going to the Archivarius solely for a sight of you, gentle lovely Serpentina!" At that moment, he felt as if Serpentina's love might be the prize of some laborious perilous task which he had to undertake; and as if this task were nothing else but the copying of the Lindhorst manuscripts. That at his very entrance into the house, or more properly, before his entrance, all sorts of mysterious things might happen, as before, was no more than he anticipated. He thought no more of Conradi's strong drink, but hastily put the vial of liquor in his waistcoat pocket, that he might act strictly by the Archivarius' directions, should the bronze Apple-woman again take it upon her to make faces at him.

And the hawk-nose actually did peak itself, the cat-eyes actually did glare from the knocker, as he raised his hand to it, at the stroke of twelve. But now, without farther ceremony, he dribbled his liquor into the pestilent visage; and it folded and moulded itself, that instant, down to a glittering bowl-round knocker. The door opened, the bells sounded beautifully over all the house: "Klingling, youngling, in, in, spring, spring, klingling." In good heart he mounted the fine broad stair; and feasted on the odours of some strange perfume that was floating through the house. In doubt, he paused in the hall; for he did not know at which of these many fine doors he was to knock. But Archivarius Lindhorst, in a white damask nightgown, emerged and said: "Well, it is a real pleasure to me, Herr Anselmus, that you have kept your word at last. Come this way, if you please; I must take you straight into the laboratory." And with this he stepped rapidly through the hall, and opened a little side door, which led into a long passage. Anselmus walked on in high spirits, behind the Archivarius; they passed from this corridor into a hall, or rather into a lordly greenhouse: for on both sides, up to the ceiling, grew all sorts of rare wondrous flowers, indeed, great trees with strangely formed leaves and blossoms. A magic dazzling light shone over the whole, though you could not discover where it came from, for no window whatever was to be seen. As the Student Anselmus looked in through the bushes and trees, long avenues appeared to open into remote distance. In the deep shade of thick cypress groves lay glittering marble fountains, out of which rose wondrous figures, spouting crystal jets that fell with pattering spray into the gleaming lily-cups. Strange voices cooed and rustled through the wood of curious trees; and sweetest perfumes streamed up and down.

The Archivarius had vanished: and Anselmus saw nothing but a huge bush of glowing fire-lilies before him. Intoxicated with the sight and the fine odours of this fairy-garden, Anselmus stood fixed to the spot. Then began on all sides of him a giggling and laughing; and light little voices railed at him and mocked him: "Herr Studiosus! Herr Studiosus! how did you get in here? Why have you dressed so bravely, Herr Anselmus? Will you chat with us for a minute and tell us how grandmamma sat down upon the egg, and young master got a stain on his Sunday waistcoat?—Can you play the new tune, now, which you learned from Daddy Cockadoodle, Herr Anselmus?—You look very fine in your glass periwig, and brown-paper boots." So cried and chattered and sniggered the little voices, out of every corner, indeed, close by the Student himself, who now observed that all sorts of multicoloured birds were fluttering above him, and jeering at him. At that moment, the bush of fire-lilies advanced towards him; and he perceived that it was Archivarius Lindhorst, whose flowered nightgown, glittering in red and yellow, had deceived his eyes.

"I beg your pardon, worthy Herr Anselmus," said the Archivarius, "for leaving you alone: I wished, in passing, to take a peep at my fine cactus, which is to blossom tonight. But how do you like my little house-garden?"

"Ah, Heaven! It is inconceivably beautiful, Herr Archivarius," replied the Student; "but these multicoloured birds have been bantering me a little."

"What chattering is this?" cried the Archivarius angrily into the bushes. Then a huge gray Parrot came fluttering out, and perched itself beside the Archivarius on a myrtle bough, and looking at him with an uncommon earnestness and gravity through a pair of spectacles that stuck on its hooked bill, it creaked out: "Don't take it amiss, Herr Archivarius; my wild boys have been a little free or so; but the Herr Studiosus has himself to blame in the matter, for——"

"Hush! hush!" interrupted Archivarius Lindhorst; "I know the varlets; but you must keep them in better discipline, my friend!— Now, come along, Herr Anselmus."

And the Archivarius again stepped forth through many a strangely decorated chamber, so that the Student Anselmus, in following him, could scarcely give a glance at all the glittering wondrous furniture and other unknown things with which all the rooms were filled. At last they entered a large apartment, where the Archivarius, casting his eyes aloft, stood still; and Anselmus got time to feast himself on the glorious sight, which the simple decoration of this hall afforded. Jutting from the azure-coloured walls rose gold-bronze trunks of high palm-trees, which wove their colossal leaves, glittering like bright emeralds, into a ceiling far up: in the middle of the chamber, and resting on three Egyptian lions, cast out of dark bronze, lay a porphyry plate; and on this stood a simple flower pot made of gold, from which, as soon as he beheld it, Anselmus could not turn away his eyes. It was as if, in a thousand gleaming reflections, all sorts of shapes were sporting on the bright polished gold: often he perceived his own form, with arms stretched out in longing—ah! beneath the elder-bush—and Serpentina was winding and shooting up and down, and again looking at him with her kind eyes. Anselmus was beside himself with frantic rapture.

"Serpentina! Serpentina!" he cried aloud; and Archivarius Lindhorst whirled round abruptly, and said: "What, Herr Anselmus? If I am not wrong, you were pleased to call for my daughter; she is in the other side of the house at present, and indeed taking her lesson on the harpsichord. Let us go along."

Anselmus, scarcely knowing what he did, followed his conductor; he saw or heard nothing more till Archivarius Lindhorst suddenly grasped his hand and said: "Here is the place!" Anselmus awoke as from a dream and now perceived that he was in a high room lined on all sides with bookshelves, and nowise differing from a common library and study. In the middle stood a large writing table, with a stuffed armchair before it. "This," said Archivarius Lindhorst, "is your workroom for the present: whether you may work, some other time, in the blue library, where you so suddenly called out my daughter's name, I do not know yet. But now I would like to convince myself of your ability to execute this task appointed you, in the way I wish it and need it." The Student here gathered full courage; and not without internal self-complacence in the certainty of highly gratifying Archivarius Lindhorst, pulled out his drawings and specimens of penmanship from his pocket. But no sooner had the Archivarius cast his eye on the first leaf, a piece of writing in the finest English style, than he smiled very oddly and shook his head. These motions he repeated at every succeeding leaf, so that the Student Anselmus felt the blood mounting to his face, and at last, when the smile became quite sarcastic and contemptuous, he broke out in downright vexation: "The Herr Archivarius does not seem contented with my poor talents."

"My dear Herr Anselmus," said Archivarius Lindhorst, "you have indeed fine capacities for the art of calligraphy; but, in the meanwhile, it is clear enough, I must reckon more on your diligence and good-will, than on your attainments."

The Student Anselmus spoke at length of his often-acknowledged perfection in this art, of his fine Chinese ink, and most select crow-quills. But Archivarius Lindhorst handed him the English sheet, and said: "Be the judge yourself!" Anselmus felt as if struck by a thunderbolt, to see the way his handwriting looked: it was miserable, beyond measure. There was no rounding in the turns, no hair-stroke where it should be; no proportion between the capital and single letters; indeed, villainous schoolboy pot-hooks often spoiled the best lines. "And then," continued Archivarius Lindhorst, "your ink will not last." He dipped his finger in a glass of water, and as he just skimmed it over the lines, they vanished without a trace. The Student Anselmus felt as if some monster were throttling him: he could not utter a word. There stood he, with the unfortunate sheet in his hand; but Archivarius Lindhorst laughed aloud, and said: "Never mind, Herr Anselmus; what you could not do well before you will perhaps do better here. At any rate, you shall have better materials than you have been accustomed to. Begin, in Heaven's name!"

From a locked press, Archivarius Lindhorst now brought out a black fluid substance, which diffused a most peculiar odour; also pens, sharply pointed and of strange colour, together with a sheet of special whiteness and smoothness; then at last an Arabic manuscript: and as Anselmus sat down to work, the Archivarius left the room. The Student Anselmus had often copied Arabic manuscripts before; the first problem, therefore, seemed to him not so very difficult to solve. "How those pot-hooks came into my fine English script, heaven and Archivarius Lindhorst know best," said he; "but that they are not from *my* hand, I will testify to the death!" At every new word that stood fair and perfect on the parchment, his courage increased, and with it his adroitness. In truth, these pens wrote exquisitely well; and the mysterious ink flowed pliantly, and black as jet, on the bright white parchment. And as he worked along so diligently, and with such strained attention, he began to feel more and more at home in the solitary room; and already he had quite fitted himself into his task, which he now hoped to finish well, when at the stroke of three the Archivarius called him into the side room to a savoury dinner. At table, Archivarius Lindhorst was in an especially good humour. He inquired about the Student Anselmus' friends, Conrector Paulmann and Registrator Heerbrand, and of the latter he had a store of merry anecdotes to tell. The good old Rhenish was particularly pleasing to the Student Anselmus, and made him more talkative than he usually was. At the stroke of four, he rose to resume his labour; and this punctuality appeared to please the Archivarius.

If the copying of these Arabic manuscripts had prospered in his hands before dinner, the task now went forward much better; indeed, he could not himself comprehend the rapidity and ease with which he succeeded in transcribing the twisted strokes of this foreign character. But it was as if, in his inmost soul, a voice were whispering in audible words: "Ah! could you accomplish it, if you were not thinking of *her*, if you did not believe in *her* and in her love?" Then there floated whispers, as in low, low, waving crystal tones, through the room: "I am near, near, near! I help you: be bold, be steadfast, dear Anselmus! I toil with you so that you may be mine!" And as, in the fullness of secret rapture, he caught these sounds, the unknown characters grew clearer and clearer to him;

he scarcely needed to look at the original at all; nay, it was as if the letters were already standing in pale ink on the parchment, and he had nothing more to do but mark them black. So did he labour on, encompassed with dear inspiring tones as with soft sweet breath, till the clock struck six and Archivarius Lindhorst entered the apartment. He came forward to the table, with a singular smile; Anselmus rose in silence: the Archivarius still looked at him, with that mocking smile: but no sooner had he glanced over the copy, than the smile passed into deep solemn earnestness, which every feature of his face adapted itself to express. He seemed no longer the same. His eyes which usually gleamed with sparkling fire, now looked with unutterable mildness at Anselmus; a soft red tinted the pale cheeks; and instead of the irony which at other times compressed the mouth, the softly curved graceful lips now seemed to be opening for wise and soul-persuading speech. His whole form was higher, statelier; the wide nightgown spread itself like a royal mantle in broad folds over his breast and shoulders; and through the white locks, which lay on his high open brow, there wound a thin band of gold.

"Young man," began the Archivarius in solemn tone, "before you were aware of it, I knew you, and all the secret relations which bind you to the dearest and holiest of my interests! Serpentina loves you; a singular destiny, whose fateful threads were spun by enemies, is fulfilled, should she become yours and if you obtain, as an essential dowry, the Golden Flower Pot, which of right belongs to her. But only from effort and contest can your happiness in the higher life arise; hostile Principles assail you; and only the interior force with which you withstand these contradictions can save you from disgrace and ruin. While labouring here, you are undergoing a season of instruction: belief and full knowledge will lead you to the near goal, if you but hold fast, what you have begun well. Bear *her* always and truly in your thoughts, her who loves you; then you will see the marvels of the Golden Pot, and be happy forevermore. Farewell! Archivarius Lindhorst expects you tomorrow at noon in his cabinet. Farewell!" With these words Archivarius Lindhorst softly pushed the Student Anselmus out of the door, which he then locked; and Anselmus found himself in the chamber where he had dined, the single door of which led out to the hallway.

Completely stupefied by these strange phenomena, the Student Anselmus stood lingering at the street door; he heard a window open above him, and looked up: it was Archivarius Lindhorst, quite the old man again, in his light-gray gown, as he usually appeared.

The Archivarius called to him: "Hey, worthy Herr Anselmus, what are you studying over there? Tush, the Arabic is still in your head. My compliments to Herr Conrector Paulmann, if you see him; and come tomorrow precisely at noon. The fee for this day is lying in your right waistcoat pocket." The Student Anselmus actually found the speziesthaler in the pocket indicated; but he derived no pleasure from it. "What is to come of all this," said he to himself, "I do not know: but if it is some mad delusion and conjuring work that has laid hold of me, my dear Serpentina still lives and moves in my inward heart; and before I leave her, I will die; for I know that the thought in me is eternal, and no hostile Principle can take it from me: and what else is this thought but Serpentina's love?"

SEVENTH VIGIL

At last Conrector Paulmann knocked the ashes out of his pipe, and said: "Now, then, it is time to go to bed." "Yes, indeed," replied Veronica, frightened at her father's sitting so late: for ten had struck long ago. No sooner, accordingly, had the Conrector withdrawn to his study and bedroom, and Fränzchen's heavy breathing signified that she was asleep, than Veronica, who to save appearances had also gone to bed, rose softly, softly, out of it again, put on her clothes, threw her mantle round her, and glided out of doors.

Ever since the moment when Veronica had left old Liese, Anselmus had continually stood before her eyes; and it seemed as if a voice that was strange to her kept repeating in her soul that he was reluctant because he was held prisoner by an enemy and that Veronica, by secret means of the magic art, could break these bonds. Her confidence in old Liese grew stronger every day; and even the impression of unearthliness and horror by degrees became less, so that all the mystery and strangeness of her relation to the crone appeared before her only in the colour of something singular, romantic, and so not a little attractive. Accordingly, she had a firm purpose, even at the risk of being missed from home, and encountering a thousand inconveniences, to undertake the adventure of the Equinox. And now, at last, the fateful night, in which old Liese had promised to afford comfort and help, had come; and Veronica, long used to thoughts of nightly wandering, was full of heart and hope. She sped through the solitary streets; heedless of the storm which was howling in the air and dashing thick raindrops in her face.

With a stifled droning clang, the Kreuzthurm clock struck eleven, as Veronica, quite wet, reached old Liese's house. "Are you here, dear! wait, love; wait, love—" cried a voice from above; and in a moment the crone, laden with a basket, and attended by her cat, was also standing at the door. "We will go, then, and do what is proper, and can prosper in the night, which favours the work." So speaking, the crone with her cold hand seized the shivering Veronica, to whom she gave the heavy basket to carry, while she herself produced a little cauldron, a trivet, and a spade. By the time they reached the open fields, the rain had ceased, but the storm had become louder; howlings in a thousand tones were flitting through the air. A horrible heart-piercing lamentation sounded down from the black clouds, which rolled themselves together in rapid flight and veiled all things in thickest darkness. But the crone stepped briskly forward, crying in a shrill harsh voice: "Light, light, my lad!" Then blue forky gleams went quivering and sputtering before them; and Veronica perceived that it was the cat emitting sparks, and bounding forward to light the way; while his doleful ghastly screams were heard in the momentary pauses of the storm. Her heart almost failed; it was as if ice-cold talons were clutching into her soul; but, with a strong effort, she collected herself, pressed closer to the crone, and said: "It must all be accomplished now, come of it what may!"

"Right, right, little daughter!" replied the crone; "be steady, like a good girl; you shall have something pretty, and Anselmus to boot."

At last the crone paused, and said: "Here is the place!" She dug a hole in the ground, then shook coals into it, put the trivet over them, and placed the cauldron on top of it. All this she accompanied with strange gestures, while the cat kept circling round her. From his tail there sputtered sparkles, which united into a ring of fire. The coals began to burn; and at last blue flames rose up around the cauldron. Veronica was ordered to lay off her mantle and veil, and to cower down beside the crone, who seized her hands, and pressed them hard, glaring with her fiery eyes at the maiden. Before long the strange materials (whether flowers, metals, herbs, or beasts, you could not determine), which the crone had taken from her basket and thrown into the cauldron, began to seethe and foam. The crone let go Veronica, then clutched an iron ladle, and plunged it into the glowing mass, which she began to stir, while Veronica, as she directed, was told to look steadfastly into the cauldron and fix her thoughts on Anselmus. Now the crone threw fresh ingredients, glittering pieces of metal, a lock of hair which Veronica had cut from her head, and a little ring which she had long worn, into the pot, while the old woman howled in dread yelling tones through the gloom, and the cat, in quick, incessant motion, whimpered and whined—

I wish very much, favorable reader, that on this twenty-third of September, you had been on the road to Dresden. In vain, when night sank down upon you, the people at the last stage-post tried to keep you there; the friendly host represented to you that the storm and the rain were too bitter, and moreover, for unearthly reasons, it was not safe to rush out into the dark on the night of the Equinox; but you paid no heed to him, thinking to yourself, "I will give the postillion a whole thaler as a tip, and so, at latest, by one o'clock I shall reach Dresden. There in the Golden Angel or the Helmet or the City of Naumburg a good supper and a soft bed await me."

And now as you ride toward Dresden through the dark, you suddenly observe in the distance a very strange, flickering light. As you come nearer, you can distinguish a ring of fire, and in its center, beside a pot out of which a thick vapour is mounting with quivering red flashes and sparkles, there sit two very different forms. Right through the fire your road leads, but the horses snort, and stamp, and rear; the postillion curses and prays, and does not spare his whip; the horses will not stir from the spot. Without thinking, you leap out of the stagecoach and hasten forward toward the fire.

And now you clearly see a pretty girl, obviously of gentle birth, who is kneeling by the cauldron in a thin white nightdress. The storm has loosened her braids, and her long chestnut-brown hair is floating freely in the wind. Full in the dazzling light from the flame flickering from beneath the trivet hovers her sweet face; but in the horror which has poured over it like an icy stream, it is stiff and pale as death; and by her updrawn eyebrows, by her mouth, which is vainly opened for the shriek of anguish which cannot find its way from her bosom compressed with unnamable torment— you perceive her terror, her horror. She holds her small soft hands aloft, spasmodically pressed together, as if she were calling with prayers her guardian angel to deliver her from the monsters of the Pit, which, in obedience to this potent spell are to appear at any moment! There she kneels, motionless as a figure of marble. Opposite her a long, shrivelled, copper-yellow crone with a peaked hawk-nose and glistering cat-eyes sits cowering. From the black cloak which is huddled around her protrude her skinny naked arms; as she stirs the Hell-broth, she laughs and cries with creaking voice through the raging, bellowing storm.

I can well believe that unearthly feelings might have arisen in you, too—unacquainted though you are otherwise with fear and dread—at the aspect of this picture by Rembrandt or Hell-Breughel, taking place in actual life. Indeed, in horror, the hairs of your head might have stood on end. But your eye could not turn away from the gentle girl entangled in these infernal doings; and the electric stroke that quivered through all your nerves and fibres, kindled in you with the speed of lightning the courageous thought of defying the mysterious powers of the ring of fire; and at this thought your horror disappeared; nay, the thought itself came into being from your feelings of horror, as their product. Your heart felt as if you yourself were one of those guardian angels to whom the maiden, frightened almost to death, was praying; nay, as if you must instantly whip out your pocket pistol and without further ceremony blow the hag's brains out. But while you were thinking of all of this most vividly, you cried aloud, "Holla!" or "What the matter here?" or "What's going on there?" The postillion blew a clanging blast on his horn; the witch ladled about in her brewage, and in a trice everything vanished in thick smoke. Whether you would have found the girl, for whom you were groping in the darkness with the most heart-felt longing, I cannot say: but you surely would have destroyed the witch's spell and undone the magic circle into which Veronica had thoughtlessly entered.

Alas! Neither you, favourable reader, nor any other man either drove or walked this way, on the twenty-third of September, in the tempestuous witch-favouring night; and Veronica had to abide by the cauldron, in deadly terror, till the work was near its close. She heard, indeed, the howling and raging around her; all sorts of hateful voices bellowed and bleated, and yelled and hummed; but she did not open her eyes, for she felt that the sight of the abominations and the horrors with which she was encircled might drive her into incurable destroying madness. The hag had ceased to stir the pot: its smoke grew fainter and fainter; and at last, nothing but a light spirit-flame was burning in the bottom. Then she cried: "Veronica, my child! my darling! look into the grounds there! What do you see? What do you see?"

Veronica could not answer, yet it seemed as if all sorts of perplexing shapes were dancing and whirling in the cauldron; and suddenly, with friendly look, reaching her his hand, the Student

Anselmus rose from the cavity of the vessel. She cried aloud:
"It is Anselmus!   It is Anselmus!"

Instantly the crone turned the cock fixed at the bottom of the
cauldron, and glowing metal rushed forth, hissing and bubbling,
into a little mould which she had placed beside it. The hag now
sprang aloft, and shrieked, capering about with wild horrific
gestures: "It is done!   It is done!   Thanks, my pretty lad; did you
watch?—Pooh, pooh, he is coming!   Bite him to death!   Bite him
to death!"   But then there sounded a strong rushing through the
air: it was as if a huge eagle were pouncing down, striking round him
with his pinions; and there shouted a tremendous voice: "Hey, hey,
vermin!—It is over!   It is over!—Home with you!"   The crone
sank down with bitter howling, and Veronica's sense and recollection
forsook her.

On her returning to herself, it was broad daylight, she was lying
in her bed, and Fränzchen was standing before her with a cup of
steaming tea and saying to her: "Tell me, sister, what in all the
world ails you?   I have been standing here this hour, and you
have been lying senseless, as if in a fever, and moaning and whimpering so that we were frightened to death.   Father has not gone to his
class this morning because of you; he will be here directly with the
doctor."

Veronica took the tea in silence: and while she was drinking it, the
horrid images of the night rose vividly before her eyes.   "So it
was all nothing but a wild dream that tortured me?   Yet last night,
I surely went to that old woman; it was the twenty-third of September too?   Well, I must have been very sick last night, and so
fancied all this; and nothing has sickened me but my perpetual
thinking of Anselmus and the strange old woman who gave herself
out for Liese, but was no such thing, and only made a fool of me with
that story."

Fränzchen, who had left the room, again came in with Veronica's
mantle, all wet, in her hand.   "Look, sister," said she, "what a
sight your mantle is!   The storm last night blew open the shutters
and upset the chair where your mantle was hanging; and the rain has
come in, and wet it for you."

This speech sank heavy on Veronica's heart, for she now saw that
it was no dream which had tormented her, but that she had really
been with the witch.   Anguish and horror took hold of her at the
thought, and a fever-frost quivered through all her frame.   In
spasmodic shuddering, she drew the bedclothes close over her; but
with this, she felt something hard pressing on her breast, and on

grasping it with her hand, it seemed like a medallion: she drew it out, as soon as Fränzchen went away with the mantle; it was a little, round, bright-polished metallic mirror. "This is a present from the woman," cried she eagerly; and it was as if fiery beams were shooting from the mirror, and penetrating into her inmost soul with benignant warmth. The fever-frost was gone, and there streamed through her whole being an unutterable feeling of contentment and cheerful delight. She could not but remember Anselmus; and as she turned her thoughts more and more intensely on him, behold, he smiled on her in friendly fashion out of the mirror, like a living miniature portrait. But before long she felt as if it were no longer the image which she saw; no! but the Student Anselmus himself alive and in person. He was sitting in a stately chamber, with the strangest furniture, and diligently writing. Veronica was about to step forward, to pat his shoulder, and say to him: "Herr Anselmus, look round; it is I!" But she could not; for it was as if a fire-stream encircled him; and yet when she looked more narrowly, this fire-stream was nothing but large books with gilt leaves. At last Veronica so far succeeded that she caught Anselmus's eye: it seemed as if he needed, in gazing at her, to bethink himself who she was; but at last he smiled and said: "Ah! Is it you, dear Mademoiselle Paulmann! But why do you like now and then to take the form of a little snake?"

At these strange words, Veronica could not help laughing aloud; and with this she awoke as from a deep dream; and hastily concealed the little mirror, for the door opened, and Conrector Paulmann with Doctor Eckstein entered the room. Dr. Eckstein stepped forward to the bedside; felt Veronica's pulse with long profound study, and then said: "Ey! Ey!" Thereupon he wrote out a prescription; again felt the pulse; a second time said: "Ey! Ey!" and then left his patient. But from these disclosures of Dr. Eckstein's, Conrector Paulmann could not clearly make out what it was that ailed Veronica.

EIGHTH VIGIL

The Student Anselmus had now worked several days with Archivarius Lindhorst; these working hours were for him the happiest of his life; still encircled with lovely tones, with Serpentina's encouraging voice, he was filled and overflowed with a pure delight, which often rose to highest rapture. Every difficulty, every little care of his needy existence, had vanished from his thoughts; and in the new life, which had risen on him as in serene sunny splendour, he comprehended all the wonders of a higher world, which before had filled him with astonishment, nay, with dread. His copying proceeded rapidly and lightly; for he felt more and more as if he were writing characters long known to him; and he scarcely needed to cast his eye upon the manuscript, while copying it all with the greatest exactness.

Except at the hour of dinner, Archivarius Lindhorst seldom made his appearance; and this always precisely at the moment when Anselmus had finished the last letter of some manuscript: then the Archivarius would hand him another, and immediately leave him, without uttering a word; having first stirred the ink with a little black rod, and changed the old pens for new sharp-pointed ones. One day, when Anselmus, at the stroke of twelve, had as usual mounted the stair, he found the door through which he commonly entered, standing locked; and Archivarius Lindhorst came forward from the other side, dressed in his strange flower-figured dressing gown. He called aloud: "Today come this way, good Herr Anselmus; for we must go to the chamber where the masters of Bhagavadgita are waiting for us."

He stepped along the corridor, and led Anselmus through the same chambers and halls as at the first visit. The Student Anselmus again felt astonished at the marvellous beauty of the garden: but he now perceived that many of the strange flowers, hanging on the dark bushes, were in truth insects gleaming with lordly colours, hovering up and down with their little wings, as they danced and whirled in clusters, caressing one another with their antennae. On the other hand again, the rose and azure-coloured birds were odoriferous flowers; and the perfume which they scattered, mounted from their cups in low lovely tones, which, with the gurgling of distant fountains, and the sighing of the high groves and trees, mingled themselves into mysterious accords of a deep unutterable longing. The mock-birds, which had so jeered and flouted him before, were again fluttering to and fro over his head, and crying incessantly with their sharp small voices: "Herr Studiosus, Herr Studiosus, don't be in such a hurry! Don't peep into the clouds so! They may fall about your ears—He! He! Herr Studiosus, put your powdermantle on; cousin Screech-Owl will frizzle your toupee." And so it went along, in all manner of stupid chatter, till Anselmus left the garden.

Archivarius Lindhorst at last stepped into the azure chamber: the porphyry, with the Golden Flower Pot, was gone; instead of it, in the middle of the room, stood a table overhung with violet-coloured satin, upon which lay the writing gear already known to Anselmus; and a stuffed armchair, covered with the same sort of cloth, was placed beside it.

"Dear Herr Anselmus," said Archivarius Lindhorst, "you have now copied for me a number of manuscripts, rapidly and correctly, to my no small contentment: you have gained my confidence; but the hardest is still ahead; and that is the transcribing or rather painting of certain works, written in a peculiar character; I keep them in this room, and they can only be copied on the spot. You will, therefore, in future, work here; but I must recommend to you the greatest foresight and attention; a false stroke, or, which may Heaven forfend, a blot let fall on the original, will plunge you into misfortune."

Anselmus observed that from the golden trunks of the palm-tree, little emerald leaves projected: one of these leaves the Archivarius took hold of; and Anselmus saw that the leaf was in truth a roll of parchment, which the Archivarius unfolded, and spread out before the Student on the table. Anselmus wondered not a little at these strangely intertwisted characters; and as he looked over the many points, strokes, dashes, and twirls in the manuscript, he almost lost hope of ever copying it. He fell into deep thought on the subject.

"Be of courage, young man!" cried the Archivarius; "if you have continuing belief and true love, Serpentina will help you."

His voice sounded like ringing metal; and as Anselmus looked up in utter terror, Archivarius Lindhorst was standing before him in the kingly form, which, during the first visit, he had assumed in the library. Anselmus felt as if in his deep reverence he could not but sink on his knee; but the Archivarius stepped up the trunk of a palm-tree, and vanished aloft among the emerald leaves. The Student Anselmus perceived that the Prince of the Spirits had been speaking with him, and was now gone up to his study; perhaps intending, by the beams which some of the Planets had despatched to him as envoys, to send back word what was to become of Anselmus and Serpentina.

"It may be too," he further thought, "that he is expecting news from the springs of the Nile; or that some magician from Lapland is paying him a visit: it behooves me to set diligently about my task." And with this, he began studying the foreign characters on the roll of parchment.

The strange music of the garden sounded over him, and encircled him with sweet lovely odours; the mock-birds, too, he still heard giggling and twittering, but could not distinguish their words, a thing which greatly pleased him. At times also it was as if the leaves of the palm-trees were rustling, and as if the clear crystal tones, which Anselmus on that fateful Ascension Day had heard under the elder-bush, were beaming and flitting through the room. Wonderfully strengthened by this shining and tinkling, the Student Anselmus directed his eyes and thoughts more and more intensely on the superscription of the parchment roll; and before long he felt, as it were from his inmost soul, that the characters could denote nothing else than these words: *Of the marriage of the Salamander with the green snake.* Then resounded a louder triphony of clear crystal bells: "Anselmus! dear Anselmus!" floated to him from the leaves; and, O wonder! on the trunk of the palm-tree the green snake came winding down.

"Serpentina! Serpentina!" cried Anselmus, in the madness of highest rapture; for as he gazed more earnestly, it was in truth a lovely glorious maiden that, looking at him with those dark blue eyes, full of inexpressible longing, as they lived in his heart, was slowly gliding down to meet him. The leaves seemed to jut out and expand; on every hand were prickles sprouting from the trunk; but Serpentina twisted and wound herself deftly through them; and so drew her fluttering robe, glancing as if in changeful colours, along with her, that, plying round the dainty form, it nowhere caught on the projecting points and prickles of the palm-tree. She sat down by Anselmus on the same chair, clasping him with her arm, and pressing him towards her, so that he felt the breath which came from her lips, and the electric warmth of her frame.

"Dear Anselmus," began Serpentina, "you shall now be wholly mine; by your belief, by your love, you shall obtain me, and I will bring you the Golden Flower Pot, which shall make us both happy forevermore."

"O, kind, lovely Serpentina!" said Anselmus. "If I have you, what do I care for anything else! If you are but mine, I will joyfully give in to all the wonderful mysteries that have beset me since the moment when I first saw you."

"I know," continued Serpentina, "that the strange and mysterious things with which my father, often merely in the sport of his humour, has surrounded you have raised distrust and dread in your mind; but now, I hope, it shall be so no more; for I came at this moment to tell you, dear Anselmus, from the bottom of my heart and soul, everything, to the smallest detail, that you need to know for understanding my father, and so for seeing clearly what your relation to him and to me really is."

Anselmus felt as if he were so wholly clasped and encircled by the gentle lovely form, that only with her could he move and live, and as if it were but the beating of her pulse that throbbed through his nerves and fibres; he listened to each one of her words till it sounded in his inmost heart, and, like a burning ray, kindled in him the rapture of Heaven. He had put his arm round that daintier than dainty waist; but the changeful glistering cloth of her robe was so smooth and slippery, that it seemed to him as if she could at any moment wind herself from his arms, and glide away. He trembled at the thought.

"Ah, do not leave me, gentlest Serpentina!" cried he; "you are my life."

"Not now," said Serpentina, "till I have told you everything that in your love of me you can comprehend:

"Know then, dearest, that my father is sprung from the wondrous race of the Salamanders; and that I owe my existence to his love for the green snake. In primeval times, in the Fairyland Atlantis, the potent Spirit-prince Phosphorus bore rule; and to him the Salamanders, and other spirits of the elements, were pledged by oath. Once upon a time, a Salamander, whom he loved before all others (it was my father), chanced to be walking in the stately garden, which Phosphorus' mother had decked in the lordliest fashion with her best gifts; and the Salamander heard a tall lily singing in low tones: 'Press down thy little eyelids, till my lover, the Morning-wind, awake thee.' He walked towards it: touched by his glowing breath, the lily opened her leaves: and he saw the lily's daughter, the green snake, lying asleep in the hollow of the flower. Then was the Salamander inflamed with warm love for the fair snake; and he carried her away from the lily, whose perfumes in nameless lamentation vainly called for her beloved daughter throughout all the garden. For the Salamander had borne her into the palace of Phosphorus, and was there beseeching him: 'Wed me with my beloved, and she shall be mine forevermore.'—'Madman, what do you ask?' said the Prince of the Spirits. 'Know that once the Lily was my mistress, and bore rule with me; but the Spark, which I cast into her, threatened to annihilate the fair Lily; and only my victory over the black Dragon, whom now the Spirits of the Earth hold in fetters, maintains her, that her leaves continue strong enough to enclose this Spark, and preserve it within them. But when you clasp the green snake, your fire will consume her frame; and a new being rapidly arising from her dust, will soar away and leave you.'

"The Salamander heeded not the warning of the Spirit-prince: full of longing ardour he folded the green snake in his arms; she crumbled into ashes; a winged being, born from her dust, soared away through the sky. Then the madness of desperation caught the Salamander; and he ran through the garden, dashing forth fire and flames; and wasted it in his wild fury, till its fairest flowers and blossoms hung down, blackened and scathed; and their lamentation filled the air. The indignant Prince of the Spirits, in his wrath, laid hold of the Salamander, and said: 'Your fire has burnt out, your flames are extinguished, your rays darkened: sink down to the Spirits of the Earth; let them mock and jeer you, and keep you captive, till the Fire-elements shall again kindle, and beam up with you as with a new being from the Earth.' The poor Salamander sank down extinguished: but now the testy old earth-spirit, who was Phosphorus' gardener, came forth and said: 'Master! who has greater cause to complain of the Salamander than I? Had not all the fair flowers, which he has burnt, been decorated with my gayest metals; had I not stoutly nursed and tended them, and spent many a fair hue on their leaves? And yet I must pity the poor Salamander; for it was but love, in which you, O Master, have full often been entangled, that drove him to despair, and made him desolate the garden. Remit his too harsh punishment!'—'His fire is for the present extinguished,' said the Prince of the Spirits; 'but in the hapless time, when the speech of nature shall no longer be intelligible to degenerate man; when the spirits of the elements, banished into their own regions, shall speak to him only from afar, in faint, spent echoes; when, displaced from the harmonious circle, an infinite longing alone shall give him tidings of the land of marvels, which he once might inhabit while belief and love still dwelt in his soul: in this hapless time, the fire of the Salamander shall again kindle; but only to manhood shall he be permitted to rise, and entering wholly into man's necessitous existence, he shall learn to endure its wants and oppressions. Yet not only shall the remembrance of his first state continue with him, but he shall again rise into the sacred harmony of all Nature; he shall understand its wonders, and the power of his fellow-spirits shall stand at his behest. Then, too, in a lily-bush, shall he find the green snake again: and the fruit of his marriage with her shall be three daughters, which, to men, shall appear in the form of their mother. In the spring season these shall disport themselves in the dark elder-bush, and sound with their lovely crystal

voices.   And then if, in that needy and mean age of inward stunted-
ness, there shall be found a youth who understands their song; nay,
if one of the little snakes look at him with her kind eyes; if the look
awaken in him forecastings of the distant wondrous land, to which,
having cast away the burden of the Common, he can courageously
soar; if, with love to the snake, there rise in him belief in the wonders
of nature, nay, in his own existence amid these wonders, then the
snake shall be his.   But not till three youths of this sort have been
found and wedded to the three daughters, may the Salamander cast
away his heavy burden, and return to his brothers.'—'Permit me,
Master,' said the earth-spirit, to make these three daughters a
present, which may glorify their life with the husbands they shall
find.   Let each of them receive from me a flower pot, of the fairest
metal which I have; I will polish it with beams borrowed from the
diamond; in its glitter shall our kingdom of wonders, as it now exists
in the harmony of universal nature be imaged back in glorious
dazzling reflection; and from its interior, on the day of marriage,
shall spring forth a fire-lily, whose eternal blossoms shall encircle
the youth that is found worthy, with sweet wafting odours.   Soon
too shall he learn its speech, and understand the wonders of our
kingdom, and dwell with his beloved in Atlantis itself.'

"Thou perceivest well, dear Anselmus, that the Salamander of
whom I speak is no other than my father.   In spite of his higher
nature, he was forced to subject himself to the paltriest contradictions
of common life; and hence, indeed, often comes the wayward
humour with which he vexes many.   He has told me now and then,
that, for the inward make of mind, which the Spirit-prince Phosphorus required as a condition of marriage with me and my sisters,
men have a name at present, which, in truth, they frequently enough
misapply: they call it a childlike poetic character.   This character,
he says, is often found in youths, who, by reason of their high sim-
plicity of manners, and their total want of what is called knowledge
of the world, are mocked by the common mob.   Ah, dear Anselmus!
beneath the elder-bush, you understood my song, my look: you love
the green snake, you believe in me, and will be mine for evermore!
The fair lily will bloom forth from the Golden Flower Pot; and we
shall dwell, happy, and united, and blessed, in Atlantis together!

"Yet I must not hide from you that in its deadly battle with the
Salamanders and spirits of the earth, the black Dragon burst from
their grasp, and hurried off through the air.   Phosphorus, indeed,
again holds him in fetters; but from the black quills, which, in the
struggle, rained down on the ground, there sprang up hostile spirits,

which on all hands set themselves against the Salamanders and spirits of the earth. That woman who hates you so, dear Anselmus, and who, as my father knows full well, is striving for possession of the Golden Flower Pot; that woman owes her existence to the love of such a quill (plucked in battle from the Dragon's wing) for a certain beet beside which it dropped. She knows her origin and her power; for, in the moans and convulsions of the captive Dragon, the secrets of many a mysterious constellation are revealed to her; and she uses every means and effort to work from the outward into the inward and unseen; while my father, with the beams which shoot forth from the spirit of the Salamander, withstands and subdues her. All the baneful principles which lurk in deadly herbs and poisonous beasts, she collects; and, mixing them under favourable constellations, raises therewith many a wicked spell, which overwhelms the soul of man with fear and trembling, and subjects him to the power of those demons, produced from the Dragon when it yielded in battle. Beware of that old woman, dear Anselmus! She hates you, because your childlike pious character has annihilated many of her wicked charms. Keep true, true to me; soon you will be at the goal!"

"O my Serpentina! my own Serpentina!" cried the Student Anselmus, "how could I leave you, how should I not love you forever!" A kiss was burning on his lips; he awoke as from a deep dream: Serpentina had vanished; six o'clock was striking, and it fell heavy on his heart that today he had not copied a single stroke. Full of anxiety, and dreading reproaches from the Archivarius, he looked into the sheet; and, O wonder! the copy of the mysterious manuscript was fairly concluded; and he thought, on viewing the characters more narrowly, that the writing was nothing else but Serpentina's story of her father, the favourite of the Spirit-prince Phosphorus, in Atlantis, the land of marvels. And now entered Archivarius Lindhorst, in his light-gray surtout, with hat and staff: he looked into the parchment on which Anselmus had been writing; took a large pinch of snuff, and said with a smile: "Just as I thought! —Well, Herr Anselmus, here is your speziesthaler; we will now go to the Linkische Bath: please follow me!" The Archivarius walked rapidly through the garden, in which there was such a din of singing, whistling, talking, that the Student Anselmus was quite deafened with it, and thanked Heaven when he found himself on the street.

Scarcely had they walked twenty paces, when they met Registrator Heerbrand, who companionably joined them. At the Gate, they filled their pipes, which they had upon them: Registrator Heerbrand complained that he had left his tinder-box behind, and could not strike fire. "Fire!" cried Archivarius Lindhorst, scornfully; "here is fire enough, and to spare!" And with this he snapped his fingers, out of which came streams of sparks, and directly kindled the pipes. —"Observe the chemical knack of some men!" said Registrator Heerbrand; but the Student Anselmus thought, not without internal awe, of the Salamander and his history.

In the Linkische Bath, Registrator Heerbrand drank so much strong double beer, that at last, though usually a good-natured quiet man, he began singing student songs in squeaking tenor; he asked every-one sharply, whether he was his friend or not? and at last had to be taken home by the Student Anselmus, long after the Archivarius Lindhorst had gone his ways.

NINTH VIGIL

The strange and mysterious things which day by day befell the Student Anselmus, had entirely withdrawn him from his customary life. He no longer visited any of his friends, and waited every morning with impatience for the hour of noon, which was to unlock his paradise. And yet while his whole soul was turned to the gentle Serpentina, and the wonders of Archivarius Lindhorst's fairy king-dom, he could not help now and then thinking of Veronica; nay, often it seemed as if she came before him and confessed with blushes how heartily she loved him; how much she longed to rescue him from the phantoms, which were mocking and befooling him. At times he felt as if a foreign power, suddenly breaking in on his mind, were drawing him with resistless force to the forgotten Veronica; as if he must needs follow her whither she pleased to lead him, nay, as if he were bound to her by ties that would not break. That very night after Serpentina had first appeared to him in the form of a lovely maiden; after the wondrous secret of the Salamander's nup-tials with the green snake had been disclosed, Veronica came before him more vividly than ever. Nay, not till he awoke, was he clearly aware that he had only been dreaming; for he had felt persuaded that Veronica was actually beside him, complaining with an expres-sion of keen sorrow, which pierced through his inmost soul, that he should sacrifice her deep true love to fantastic visions, which only the distemper of his mind called into being, and which, moreover, would at last prove his ruin. Veronica was lovelier than he had ever seen her; he could not drive her from his thoughts: and in this perplexed and contradictory mood he hastened out, hoping to get rid of it by a morning walk.

A secret magic influence led him on the Pirna gate: he was just turning into a cross street, when Conrector Paulmann, coming after him, cried out: "Ey! Ey!—Dear Herr Anselmus!—*Amice! Amice!* Where, in Heaven's name, have you been buried so long? We never see you at all. Do you know, Veronica is longing very much to have another song with you. So come along; you were just on the road to me, at any rate."

The Student Anselmus, constrained by this friendly violence, went along with the Conrector. On entering the house, they were met by Veronica, attired with such neatness and attention, that Conrector Paulmann, full of amazement, asked her: "Why so decked, Mamsell? Were you expecting visitors? Well, here I bring you Herr Anselmus."

The Student Anselmus, in daintily and elegantly kissing Veronica's hand, felt a small soft pressure from it, which shot like a stream of fire over all his frame. Veronica was cheerfulness, was grace itself; and when Paulmann left them for his study, she contrived, by all manner of rogueries and waggeries, to uplift the Student Anselmus so much that he at last quite forgot his bashfulness, and jigged round the room with the playful girl. But here again the demon of awkwardness got hold of him: he jolted on a table, and Veronica's pretty little workbox fell to the floor. Anselmus lifted it; the lid had flown up; and a little round metallic mirror was glittering on him, into which he looked with peculiar delight. Veronica glided softly up to him; laid her hand on his arm, and pressing close to him, looked over his shoulder into the mirror also. And now Anselmus felt as if a battle were beginning in his soul: thoughts, images flashed out—Archivarius Lindhorst—Serpentina—the green snake —at last the tumult abated, and all this chaos arranged and shaped itself into distinct consciousness. It was now clear to him that he had always thought of Veronica alone; nay, that the form which had yesterday appeared to him in the blue chamber, had been no other than Veronica; and that the wild legend of the Salamander's marriage with the green snake had merely been written down by him from the manuscript, but nowise related in his hearing. He wondered greatly at all these dreams; and ascribed them solely to the heated state of mind into which Veronica's love had brought him, as well as to his working with Archivarius Lindhorst, in whose rooms there were, besides, so many strangely intoxicating odours. He could not help laughing heartily at the mad whim of falling in love with a little green snake; and taking a well-fed Privy Archivarius for a Salamander: "Yes, yes! It is Veronica!" cried he aloud; but on turning round his head, he looked right into Veronica's blue eyes, from which warmest love was beaming. A faint soft Ah! escaped her lips, which at that moment were burning on his.

"O happy I!" sighed the enraptured Student: "What I yester-night but dreamed, is in very deed mine today."

"But will you really marry me, then, when you are a Hofrath?" said Veronica.

"That I will," replied the Student Anselmus; and just then the door creaked, and Conrector Paulmann entered with the words:

"Now, dear Herr Anselmus, I will not let you go today. You will put up with a bad dinner; then Veronica will make us delight-ful coffee, which we shall drink with Registrator Heerbrand, for he promised to come here."

"Ah, Herr Conrector!" answered the Student Anselmus, "are you not aware that I must go to Archivarius Lindhorst's and copy?"

"Look, *Amice!*" said Conrector Paulmann, holding up his watch, which pointed to half-past twelve.

The Student Anselmus saw clearly that he was much too late for Archivarius Lindhorst; and he complied with the Conrector's wishes the more readily, as he might now hope to look at Veronica the whole day long, to obtain many a stolen glance, and little squeeze of the hand, nay, even to succeed in conquering a kiss. So high had the Student Anselmus's desires now mounted; he felt more and more contented in soul, the more fully he convinced himself that he should soon be delivered from all these fantasies, which really might have made a sheer idiot of him.

Registrator Heerbrand came, as he had promised, after dinner; and coffee being over, and the dusk come on, the Registrator, puck-ering his face together, and gaily rubbing his hands, signified that he had something about him, which, if mingled and reduced to form, as it were, paged and titled, by Veronica's fair hands, might be pleasant to them all, on this October evening.

"Come out, then, with this mysterious substance which you carry with you, most valued Registrator," cried Conrector Paulmann. Then Registrator Heerbrand shoved his hand into his deep pocket, and at three journeys, brought out a bottle of arrack, two lemons, and a quantity of sugar. Before half an hour had passed, a savoury bowl of punch was smoking on Paulmann's table. Veronica drank their health in a sip of the liquor; and before long there was plenty of gay, good-natured chat among the friends. But the Student

Anselmus, as the spirit of the drink mounted into his head, felt all the images of those wondrous things, which for some time he had experienced, again coming through his mind. He saw the Archivarius in his damask dressing gown, which glittered like phosphorus; he saw the azure room, the golden palm-trees; nay, it now seemed to him as if he must still believe in Serpentina: there was a fermentation, a conflicting tumult in his soul. Veronica handed him a glass of punch; and in taking it, he gently touched her hand. "Serpentina! Veronica!" sighed he to himself. He sank into deep dreams; but Registrator Heerbrand cried quite aloud: "A strange old gentleman, whom nobody can fathom, he is and will be, this Archivarius Lindhorst. Well, long life to him! Your glass, Herr Anselmus!"

Then the Student Anselmus awoke from his dreams, and said, as he touched glasses with Registrator Heerbrand: "That proceeds, respected Herr Registrator, from the circumstance, that Archivarius Lindhorst is in reality a Salamander, who in his fury laid waste the Spirit-prince Phosphorus' garden, because the green snake had flown away from him."

"What?" inquired Conrector Paulmann.

"Yes," continued the Student Anselmus; "and for this reason he is now forced to be a Royal Archivarius; and to keep house here in Dresden with his three daughters, who, after all, are nothing more than little gold-green snakes, that bask in elder-bushes, and traitorously sing, and seduce away young people, like so many sirens."

"Herr Anselmus! Herr Anselmus!" cried Conrector Paulmann, "is there a crack in your brain? In Heaven's name, what monstrous stuff is this you are babbling?"

"He is right," interrupted Registrator Heerbrand: "that fellow, that Archivarius, is a cursed Salamander, and strikes you fiery snips from his fingers, which burn holes in your surtout like red-hot tinder. Ay, ay, you are in the right, brotherkin Anselmus; and whoever says No, is saying No to me!" And at these words Registrator Heerbrand struck the table with his fist, till the glasses rung again.

"Registrator! Are you raving mad?" cried the enraged Conrector. "Herr Studiosus, Herr Studiosus! what is this you are about again?"

"Ah!" said the Student, "you too are nothing but a bird, a screech-owl, that frizzles toupees, Herr Conrector!"

"What?—I a bird?—A screech-owl, a frizzler?" cried the Conrector, full of indignation: "Sir, you are mad, born mad!"

"But the crone will get a clutch of him," cried Registrator Heerbrand.

"Yes, the crone is potent," interrupted the Student Anselmus, "though she is but of mean descent; for her father was nothing but a ragged wing-feather, and her mother a dirty beet: but the most of her power she owes to all sorts of baneful creatures, poisonous vermin which she keeps about her."

"That is a horrid calumny," cried Veronica, with eyes all glowing in anger: "old Liese is a wise woman; and the black cat is no baneful creature, but a polished young gentleman of elegant manners, and her cousin-german."

"Can *he* eat Salamanders without singeing his whiskers, and dying like a snuffed candle?" cried Registrator Heerbrand.

"No! no!" shouted the Student Anselmus, "that he never can in this world; and the green snake loves me, and I have looked into Serpentina's eyes."

"The cat will scratch them out," cried Veronica.

"Salamander, Salamander beats them all, all," hallooed Conrector Paulmann, in the highest fury: "But am I in a madhouse? Am I mad myself? What foolish nonsense am I chattering? Yes, I am mad too! mad too!" And with this, Conrector Paulmann started up; tore the peruke from his head, and dashed it against the ceiling of the room; till the battered locks whizzed, and, tangled into utter disorder, it rained down powder far and wide. Then the Student Anselmus and Registrator Heerbrand seized the punch-bowl and the glasses; and, hallooing and huzzaing, pitched them against the ceiling also, and the sherds fell jingling and tingling about their ears.

"*Vivat* the Salamander!—*Pereat, pereat* the crone!—Break the metal mirror!—Dig the cat's eyes out!—Bird, little bird, from the air—*Eheu—Eheu—Evoe—Evoe*, Salamander!" So shrieked, and shouted, and bellowed the three, like utter maniacs. With loud weeping, Fränzchen ran out; but Veronica lay whimpering for pain and sorrow on the sofa.

At this moment the door opened: all was instantly still; and a little man, in a small gray cloak, came stepping in. His countenance had a singular air of gravity; and especially the round hooked nose, on which was a huge pair of spectacles, distinguished itself from all noses ever seen. He wore a strange peruke too; more like a feather-cap than a wig.

"Ey, many good-evenings!" grated and cackled the little comical mannikin. "Is the Student Herr Anselmus among you, gentlemen?

—Best compliments from Archivarius Lindhorst; he has waited today in vain for Herr Anselmus; but tomorrow he begs most respectfully to request that Herr Anselmus does not miss the hour."

And with this, he went out again; and all of them now saw clearly that the grave little mannikin was in fact a gray parrot. Conrector Paulmann and Registrator Heerbrand raised a horselaugh, which reverberated through the room; and in the intervals, Veronica was moaning and whimpering, as if torn by nameless sorrow; but, as to the Student Anselmus, the madness of inward horror was darting through him; and unconsciously he ran through the door, along the streets. Instinctively he reached his house, his garret. Ere long Veronica came in to him, with a peaceful and friendly look, and asked him why, in the festivity, he had so vexed her; and desired him to be upon his guard against figments of the imagination while working at Archivarius Lindhorst's. "Goodnight, goodnight, my beloved friend!" whispered Veronica scarcely audibly, and breathed a kiss on his lips. He stretched out his arms to clasp her, but the dreamy shape had vanished, and he awoke cheerful and refreshed. He could not but laugh heartily at the effects of the punch; but in thinking of Veronica, he felt pervaded by a most delightful feeling. "To her alone," said he within himself, "do I owe this return from my insane whims. Indeed, I was little better than the man who believed himself to be of glass; or the one who did not dare leave his room for fear the hens should eat him, since he was a barleycorn. But so soon as I am Hofrath, I shall marry Mademoiselle Paulmann, and be happy, and there's an end to it."

At noon, as he walked through Archivarius Lindhorst's garden, he could not help wondering how all this had once appeared so strange and marvellous. He now saw nothing that was not common; earthen flowerpots, quantities of geraniums, myrtles, and the like. Instead of the glittering multi-coloured birds which used to flout him, there were nothing but a few sparrows, fluttering hither and thither, which raised an unpleasant unintelligible cry at sight of Anselmus. The azure room also had quite a different look; and he could not understand how that glaring blue, and those unnatural golden trunks of palm-trees, with their shapeless glistening leaves, should ever have pleased him for a moment. The Archivarius looked at him with a most peculiar ironic smile, and asked: "Well, how did you like the punch last night, good Anselmus?"

"Ah, doubtless you have heard from the gray parrot how——" answered the Student Anselmus, quite ashamed; but he stopped short, thinking that this appearance of the parrot was all a piece of jugglery.

"I was there myself," said Archivarius Lindhorst; "didn't you see me? But, among the mad pranks you were playing, I almost got lamed: for I was sitting in the punch bowl, at the very moment when Registrator Heerbrand laid hands on it, to dash it against the ceiling; and I had to make a quick retreat into the Conrector's pipe-head. Now, adieu, Herr Anselmus! Be diligent at your task; for the lost day you shall also have a speziesthaler, because you worked so well before."

"How can the Archivarius babble such mad stuff?" thought the Student Anselmus, sitting down at the table to begin the copying of the manuscript, which Archivarius Lindhorst had as usual spread out before him. But on the parchment roll, he perceived so many strange crabbed strokes and twirls all twisted together in inexplicable confusion, offering no resting point for the eye, that it seemed to him well nigh impossible to copy all this exactly. Nay, in glancing over the whole, you might have thought the parchment was nothing but a piece of thickly veined marble, or a stone sprinkled over with lichens. Nevertheless he determined to do his utmost; and boldly dipped in his pen: but the ink would not run, do what he liked; impatiently he flicked the point of his pen against his fingernail, and—Heaven and Earth!—a huge blot fell on the outspread original! Hissing and foaming, a blue flash rose from the blot; and crackling and wavering, shot through the room to the ceiling. Then a thick vapour rolled from the walls; the leaves began to rustle, as if shaken by a tempest; and down out of them darted glaring basilisks in sparkling fire; these kindled the vapour, and the bickering masses of flame rolled round Anselmus. The golden trunks of the palm-trees became gigantic snakes, which knocked their frightful heads together with piercing metallic clang; and wound their scaly bodies round Anselmus.

"Madman! suffer now the punishment of what, in capricious irreverence, thou hast done!" cried the frightful voice of the crowned Salamander, who appeared above the snakes like a glittering beam in the midst of the flame: and now the yawning jaws of the snakes poured forth cataracts of fire on Anselmus; and it was as if the fire-streams were congealing about his body, and changing into a firm ice-cold mass. But while Anselmus's limbs, more and more pressed together, and contracted, stiffened into powerlessness, his senses passed away. On returning to himself, he could not stir a joint: he was as if surrounded with a glistening brightness, on which he struck if he but tried to lift his hand.—Alas! He was sitting in a well-corked crystal bottle, on a shelf, in the library of Archivarius Lindhorst.

TENTH VIGIL

I am probably right in doubting, gracious reader, that you were ever sealed up in a glass bottle, or even that you have ever been oppressed with such sorcery in your most vivid dreams. If you have had such dreams, you will understand the Student Anselmus's woe and will feel it keenly enough; but if you have not, then your flying imagination, for the sake of Anselmus and me, will have to be obliging enough to enclose itself for a few moments in the crystal. You are drowned in dazzling splendour; everything around you appears illuminated and begirt with beaming rainbow hues: in the sheen everything seems to quiver and waver and clang and drone. You are swimming, but you are powerless and cannot move, as if you were imbedded in a firmly congealed ether which squeezes you so tightly that it is in vain that your spirit commands your dead and stiffened body. Heavier and heavier the mountainous burden lies on you; more and more every breath exhausts the tiny bit of air that still plays up and down in the tight space around you; your pulse throbs madly; and cut through with horrid anguish, every nerve is quivering and bleeding in your dead agony.

Favourable reader, have pity on the Student Anselmus! This inexpressible torture seized him in his glass prison: but he felt too well that even death could not release him, for when he had fainted with pain, he awoke again to new wretchedness when the morning sun shone into the room. He could move no limb, and his thoughts struck against the glass, stunning him with discordant clang; and instead of the words which the spirit used to speak from within him he now heard only the stifled din of madness. Then he exclaimed in his despair: "O Serpentina! Serpentina! Save me from this agony of Hell!" And it was as if faint sighs breathed around him, which spread like transparent green elder-leaves over the glass; the clanging ceased; the dazzling, perplexing glitter was gone, and he breathed more freely.

"Haven't I myself solely to blame for my misery? Ah! Haven't I sinned against you, kind, beloved Serpentina? Haven't I raised vile doubts of you? Haven't I lost my belief, and with it, all, all that was to make me so blessed? Ah! You will now never, never be mine; for me the Golden Pot is lost, and I shall not behold its wonders any more. Ah, could I but see you but once more; but once more hear your kind, sweet voice, lovely Serpentina!"

So wailed the Student Anselmus, caught with deep piercing sorrow: then a voice spoke close by him: "What the devil ails you, Herr Studiosus? What makes you lament so, out of all compass and measure?"

The Student Anselmus now perceived that on the same shelf with him were five other bottles, in which he perceived three Kreuzkirche Scholars, and two Law Clerks.

"Ah, gentlemen, my fellows in misery," cried he, "how is it possible for you to be so calm, nay, so happy, as I read in your cheerful looks? You are sitting here corked up in glass bottles, as well as I, and cannot move a finger, nay, not think a reasonable thought, but there rises such a murder-tumult of clanging and droning, and in your head itself a tumbling and rumbling enough to drive one mad. But of course you do not believe in the Salamander, or the green snake."

"You are pleased to jest, Mein Herr Studiosus," replied a Kreuzkirche Scholar; "we have never been better off than at present: for the speziesthalers which the mad Archivarius gave us for all kinds of pot-hook copies, are chinking in our pockets; we have now no Italian choruses to learn by heart; we go every day to Joseph's or other beer gardens, where the double-beer is sufficient, and we can look a pretty girl in the face; so we sing like real Students, *Gaudeamus igitur*, and are contented!"

"They of the Cross are quite right," added a Law Clerk; "I too am well furnished with speziesthalers, like my dearest colleague beside me here; and we now diligently walk about on the Weinberg, instead of scurvy law-copying within four walls."

"But, my best, worthiest masters!" said the Student Anselmus, "do you not observe, then, that you are all and sundry corked up in glass bottles, and cannot for your hearts walk a hairsbreadth?"

Here the Kreuzkirche Scholars and the Law Clerks set up a loud laugh, and cried: "The Student is mad; he fancies himself to be sitting in a glass bottle, and is standing on the Elbe Bridge and looking right down into the water. Let us go on our way!"

"Ah!" sighed the Student, "they have never seen the kind Serpentina; they do not know what Freedom, and life in Love, and Belief, signify; and so by reason of their folly and low-mindedness, they do not feel the oppression of the imprisonment into which the Salamander has cast them. But I, unhappy I, must perish in want and woe, if she whom I so inexpressibly love does not rescue me!"

Then, waving in faint tinkles, Serpentina's voice flitted through the room: "Anselmus! Believe, love, hope!" And every tone beamed into Anselmus's prison; and the crystal yielded to his pressure and expanded, till the breast of the captive could move and heave.

The torment of his situation became less and less, and he saw clearly that Serpentina still loved him; and that it was she alone, who had rendered his confinement tolerable. He disturbed himself no more about his inane companions in misfortune; but directed all his thoughts and meditations on the gentle Serpentina. Suddenly, however, there arose on the other side a dull, croaking repulsive murmur. Before long he could observe that it came from an old coffeepot, with half-broken lid, standing opposite him on a little shelf. As he looked at it more narrowly, the ugly features of a wrinkled old woman unfolded themselves gradually; and in a few moments the Apple-wife of the Schwarzthor stood before him. She grinned and laughed at him, and cried with screeching voice: "Ey, ey, my pretty boy, must you lie in limbo now? In the crystal you ended! Didn't I tell you so long ago?"

"Mock and jeer me, you cursed witch!" said Anselmus, "you are to blame for it all; but the Salamander will catch you, you vile beet!"

"Ho, ho!" replied the crone, "not so proud, my fine copyist. You have squashed my little sons and you have scarred my nose; but I still love you, you knave, for once you were a pretty fellow, and my little daughter likes you, too. Out of the crystal you will never get unless I help you: I cannot climb up there, but my friend the rat, that lives close behind you, will eat the shelf in two; you will jingle down, and I shall catch you in my apron so that your nose doesn't get broken or your fine sleek face get injured at all. Then I will carry you to Mamsell Veronica, and you shall marry her when you become Hofrath."

"Get away, you devil's brood!" shouted the Student Anselmus in fury. "It was you alone and your hellish arts that made me commit the sin which I must now expiate. But I will bear it all patiently: for only here can I be encircled with Serpentina's love and consolation. Listen to me, you hag, and despair! I defy your power: I love Serpentina and none but her forever. I will not become Hofrath, I will not look at Veronica; by your means she is enticing me to evil. If the green snake cannot be mine, I will die in sorrow and longing. Away, filthy buzzard!"

The crone laughed, till the chamber rang: "Sit and die then," cried she: "but now it is time to set to work; for I have other trade to follow here." She threw off her black cloak, and so stood in hideous nakedness; then she ran round in circles, and large folios came tumbling down to her; out of these she tore parchment leaves, and rapidly patching them together in artful combination, and fixing them on her body, in a few instants she was dressed as if in strange multi-colored armor. Spitting fire, the black cat darted out of the ink-glass, which was standing on the table, and ran mewing towards the crone, who shrieked in loud triumph, and along with him vanished through the door.

Anselmus observed that she went towards the azure chamber; and directly he heard a hissing and storming in the distance; the birds in the garden were crying; the Parrot creaked out: "Help! help! Thieves! thieves!" That moment the crone returned with a bound into the room, carrying the Golden Flower Pot on her arm, and with hideous gestures, shrieking wildly through the air; "Joy! joy, little son!—Kill the green snake! To her, son! To her!"

Anselmus thought he heard a deep moaning, heard Serpentina's voice. Then horror and despair took hold of him: he gathered all his force, he dashed violently, as if every nerve and artery were bursting, against the crystal; a piercing clang went through the room, and the Archivarius in his bright damask dressing gown was standing in the door.

"Hey, hey! vermin!—Mad spell!—Witchwork!—Here, holla!" So shouted he: then the black hair of the crone started up in tufts; her red eyes glanced with infernal fire, and clenching together the peaked fangs of her abominable jaws, she hissed: "Hiss, at him! Hiss, at him! Hiss!" and laughed and neighed in scorn and mockery, and pressed the Golden Flower Pot firmly to her, and threw out of it handfuls of glittering earth on the Archivarius; but as it touched the dressing gown, the earth changed into flowers, which rained down on the ground. Then the lilies of the dressing gown flickered and flamed up; and the Archivarius caught these lilies blazing in sparky fire and dashed them on the witch; she howled with agony, but as she leaped aloft and shook her armor of parchment the lilies went out, and fell away into ashes.

"To her, my lad!" creaked the crone: then the black cat darted through the air, and bounded over the Archivarius's head towards the door; but the gray parrot fluttered out against him; caught him by the nape with his crooked bill, till red fiery blood burst down over his neck; and Serpentina's voice cried: "Saved! Saved!" Then the crone, foaming with rage and desperation, darted at the Archivarius: she threw the Golden Flower Pot behind her, and holding up the long talons of her skinny fists, tried to clutch the Archivarius by the throat: but he instantly doffed his dressing gown, and hurled it against her. Then, hissing, and sputtering, and bursting, blue flames shot from the parchment leaves, and the crone rolled around howling in agony, and strove to get fresh earth from the Flower Pot, fresh parchment leaves from the books, that she might stifle the blazing flames; and whenever any earth or leaves came down on her, the flames went out. But now, from the interior of the Archivarius issued fiery crackling beams, which darted on the crone.

"Hey, hey! To it again! Salamander! Victory!" clanged the Archivarius's voice through the chamber; and a hundred bolts whirled forth in fiery circles round the shrieking crone. Whizzing and buzzing flew cat and parrot in their furious battle; but at last the parrot, with his strong wing, dashed the cat to the ground; and with his talons transfixing and holding fast his adversary, which, in deadly agony, uttered horrid mews and howls, he, with his sharp bill, picked out his glowing eyes, and the burning froth spouted from them. Then thick vapour streamed up from the spot where the crone, hurled to the ground, was lying under the dressing gown: her howling, her terrific, piercing cry of lamentation, died away in the remote distance. The smoke, which had spread abroad with penetrating stench, cleared away; the Archivarius picked up his dressing gown; and under it lay an ugly beet.

"Honoured Herr Archivarius, here let me offer you the vanquished foe," said the parrot, holding out a black hair in his beak to Archivarius Lindhorst.

"Very right, my worthy friend," replied the Archivarius: "here lies my vanquished foe too: be so good now as manage what remains. This very day, as a small douceur, you shall have six coconuts, and a new pair of spectacles also, for I see the cat has villainously broken the glasses of these old ones."

"Yours forever, most honoured friend and patron!" answered the parrot, much delighted; then took the withered beet in his bill, and fluttered out with it by the window, which Archivarius Lindhorst had opened for him.

The Archivarius now lifted the Golden Flower Pot, and cried, with a strong voice, "Serpentina! Serpentina!" But as the Student Anselmus, rejoicing in the destruction of the vile witch who had hurried him into misfortune, cast his eyes on the Archivarius, behold, here stood once more the high majestic form of the Spirit-prince, looking up to him with indescribable dignity and grace. "Anselmus," said the Spirit-prince, "not you, but a hostile principle, which strove destructively to penetrate into your nature, and divide you against yourself, was to blame for your unbelief. You have kept your faithfulness: be free and happy." A bright flash quivered through the spirit of Anselmus: the royal triphony of the crystal bells sounded stronger and louder than he had ever heard it: his nerves and fibres thrilled; but, swelling higher and higher, the melodious tones rang through the room; the glass which enclosed Anselmus broke; and he rushed into the arms of his dear and gentle Serpentina.

ELEVENTH VIGIL

"But tell me, best Registrator! how could the cursed punch last night mount into our heads, and drive us to all kinds of *allotria*?" So said Conrector Paulmann, as he next morning entered his room, which still lay full of broken sherds; with his hapless peruke, dissolved into its original elements, soaked in punch among the ruin. For after the Student Anselmus ran out, Conrector Paulmann and Registrator Heerbrand had kept trotting and hobbling up and down the room, shouting like maniacs, and butting their heads together; till Fränzchen, with much labour, carried her dizzy papa to bed; and Registrator Heerbrand, in the deepest exhaustion, sank on the sofa, which Veronica had left, taking refuge in her bedroom. Registrator Heerbrand had his blue handkerchief tied about his head; he looked quite pale and melancholic, and moaned out: "Ah, worthy Conrector, it was not the punch which Mamsell Veronica most admirably brewed, no! but it was simply that cursed Student who was to blame for all the mischief. Do you not observe that he has long been *mente captus*? And are you not aware that madness is infectious? One fool makes twenty; pardon me, it is an old proverb: especially when you have drunk a glass or two, you fall into madness quite readily, and then involuntarily you manoeuvre, and go through your exercise, just as the crack-brained fugleman makes the motion. Would you believe it, Conrector? I am still giddy when I think of that gray parrot!"

"Gray fiddlestick!" interrupted the Conrector: "it was nothing but Archivarius Lindhorst's little old Famulus, who had thrown a gray cloak over himself, and was looking for the Student Anselmus."

"It may be," answered Registrator Heerbrand; "but, I must confess, I am quite downcast in spirit; the whole night through there was such a piping and organing."

"That was I," said the Conrector, "for I snore loud."

"Well, may be," answered the Registrator: "but, Conrector, Conrector! I had reason to raise some cheerfulness among us last night—And that Anselmus spoiled it all! You do not know—O Conrector, Conrector!" And with this, Registrator Heerbrand started up; plucked the cloth from his head, embraced the Conrector, warmly pressed his hand, and again cried, in quite heart-breaking tone: "O Conrector, Conrector!" and snatching his hat and staff, rushed out of doors.

"This Anselmus will not cross my threshold again," said Conrector Paulmann; "for I see very well, that, with this moping madness of his, he robs the best gentlemen of their senses. The Registrator has now gone overboard, too: I have hitherto kept safe; but the Devil, who knocked hard last night in our carousal, may get in at last, and play his tricks with me. So *Apage, Satanas!* Off with thee, Anselmus!" Veronica had grown quite pensive; she spoke no word; only smiled now and then very oddly, and seemed to wish to be left alone. "She, too, has Anselmus in her head," said the Conrector, full of spleen: "but it is well that he does not show himself here; I know he fears me, this Anselmus, and so he will never come."

These concluding words Conrector Paulmann spoke aloud; then the tears rushed into Veronica's eyes, and she said, sobbing: "Ah! how can Anselmus come? He has been corked up in the glass bottle for a long time."

"What? What?" cried Conrector Paulmann. "Ah Heaven! Ah Heaven! she is doting too, like the Registrator: the loud fit will soon come! Ah, you cursed, abominable, thrice-cursed Anselmus!" He ran forth directly to Dr. Eckstein; who smiled, and again said: "Ey! Ey!" This time, however, he prescribed nothing; but added, to the little he had uttered, the following words, as he walked away: "Nerves! Come round of itself. Take the air; walks; amusements; theatre; playing *Sonntagskind, Schwestern von Prag.* Come around of itself."

"I have seldom seen the Doctor so eloquent," thought Conrector Paulmann; "really talkative, I declare!"

Several days and weeks and months passed. Anselmus had vanished; but Registrator Heerbrand did not make his appearance either: not till the fourth of February, when, in a fashionable new

coat of the finest cloth, in shoes and silk stockings, notwithstanding
the keen frost, and with a large nosegay of fresh flowers in his hand,
the Registrator entered precisely at noon the parlour of Conrector
Paulmann, who wondered not a little to see his friend so well
dressed.   With a solemn air, Registrator Heerbrand came forward
to Conrector Paulmann; embraced him with the finest elegance,
and then said: "Now at last, on the Saint's-day of your beloved and
most honoured Mamsell Veronica, I will tell you out, straightforward,
what I have long had lying at my heart.   That evening, that unfortunate evening, when I put the ingredients of our noxious punch
in my pocket, I intended to tell to you a piece of good news, and to
celebrate the happy day in convivial joys.   I had learned that I
was to be made Hofrath; for which promotion I have now the patent,
cum nomine et sigillo Principis, in my pocket."

"Ah! Herr Registr—Herr Hofrath Heerbrand, I meant to say,"
stammered the Conrector.

"But it is you, most honoured Conrector," continued the new
Hofrath; "it is you alone that can complete my happiness.   For a
long time, I have in secret loved your daughter, Mamsell Veronica;
and I can boast of many a kind look which she has given me,
evidently showing that she would not reject me.   In one word,
honoured Conrector! I, Hofrath Heerbrand, do now entreat of you
the hand of your most amiable Mamsell Veronica, whom I, if you
have nothing against it, purpose shortly to take home as my
wife."

Conrector Paulmann, full of astonishment, clapped his hands
repeatedly, and cried: "Ey, Ey, Ey!   Herr Registr—Herr Hofrath,
I meant to say—who would have thought it?   Well, if Veronica
does really love you, I for my share cannot object: nay, perhaps,
her present melancholy is nothing but concealed love for you, most
honoured Hofrath!   You know what freaks women have!"

At this moment Veronica entered, pale and agitated, as she now
commonly was.   Then Hofrath Heerbrand approached her; men-
tioned in a neat speech her Saint's-day, and handed her the odorous
nosegay, along with a little packet; out of which, when she opened
it, a pair of glittering earrings gleamed up at her.   A rapid flying
blush tinted her cheeks; her eyes sparkled in joy, and she cried:
"O Heaven!   These are the very earrings which I wore some weeks
ago, and thought so much of."

"How can this be, dearest Mamsell," interrupted Hofrath Heerbrand, somewhat alarmed and hurt, "when I bought them not an
hour ago, in the Schlossgasse, for cash?"

But Veronica paid no attention to him; she was standing before the mirror to witness the effect of the trinkets, which she had already suspended in her pretty little ears. Conrector Paulmann disclosed to her, with grave countenance and solemn tone, his friend Heerbrand's preferment and present proposal. Veronica looked at the Hofrath with a searching look, and said: "I have long known that you wished to marry me. Well, be it so! I promise you my heart and hand; but I must now unfold to you, to both of you, I mean, my father and my bridegroom, much that is lying heavy on my heart; yes, even now, though the soup should get cold, which I see Fränzchen is just putting on the table."

Without waiting for the Conrector's or the Hofrath's reply, though the words were visibly hovering on the lips of both, Veronica continued: "You may believe me, father, I loved Anselmus from my heart, and when Registrator Heerbrand, who is now become Hofrath himself, assured us that Anselmus might possibly rise that high, I resolved that he and no other should be my husband. But then it seemed as if alien hostile beings tried snatching him away from me: I had recourse to old Liese, who was once my nurse, but is now a wise woman, and a great enchantress. She promised to help me, and give Anselmus wholly into my hands. We went at midnight on the Equinox to the crossing of the roads: she conjured certain hellish spirits, and by aid of the black cat, we manufactured a little metallic mirror, in which I, directing my thoughts on Anselmus, had but to look, in order to rule him wholly in heart and mind. But now I heartily repent having done all this; and here abjure all Satanic arts. The Salamander has conquered old Liese; I heard her shrieks; but there was no help to be given: so soon as the parrot had eaten the beet, my metallic mirror broke in two with a piercing clang." Veronica took out both the pieces of the mirror, and a lock of hair from her workbox, and handing them to Hofrath Heerbrand, she proceeded: "Here, take the fragments of the mirror, dear Hofrath; throw them down, tonight, at twelve o'clock, over the Elbe Bridge, from the place where the Cross stands; the stream is not frozen there: the lock, however, wear on your faithful breast. I here abjure all magic: and heartily wish Anselmus joy of his good fortune, seeing he is wedded with the green snake, who is much prettier and richer than I. You dear Hofrath, I will love and reverence as becomes a true honest wife."

"Alack! Alack!" cried Conrector Paulmann, full of sorrow; "she is cracked, she is cracked; she can never be Frau Hofräthinn; she is cracked!"

"Not in the smallest," interrupted Hofrath Heerbrand; "I know well that Mamsell Veronica has had some kindness for the loutish Anselmus; and it may be that in some fit of passion, she has had recourse to the wise woman, who, as I perceive, can be no other than the card-caster and coffee-pourer of the Seethor; in a word, old Rauerin. Nor can it be denied that there are secret arts, which exert their influence on men but too banefully; we read of such in the ancients, and doubtless there are still such; but as to what Mamsell Veronica is pleased to say about the victory of the Salamander, and the marriage of Anselmus with the green snake, this, in reality, I take for nothing but a poetic allegory; a sort of song, wherein she sings her entire farewell to the Student."

"Take it for what you will, my dear Hofrath!" cried Veronica; "perhaps for a very stupid dream."

"That I will not do," replied Hofrath Heerbrand; "for I know well that Anselmus himself is possessed by secret powers, which vex him and drive him on to all imaginable mad escapades."

Conrector Paulmann could stand it no longer; he burst out: "Hold! For the love of Heaven, hold! Are we overtaken with that cursed punch again, or has Anselmus's madness come over us too? Herr Hofrath, what stuff is this you are talking? I will suppose, however, that it is love which haunts your brain: this soon comes to rights in marriage; otherwise, I should be apprehensive that you too had fallen into some shade of madness, most honoured Herr Hofrath; then what would become of the future branches of the family, inheriting the *malum* of their parents? But now I give my paternal blessing to this happy union; and permit you as bride and bridegroom to take a kiss."

This immediately took place; and thus before the soup had grown cold, a formal betrothment was concluded. In a few weeks, Frau Hofräthinn Heerbrand was actually, as she had been in vision, sitting in the balcony of a fine house in the Neumarkt, and looking down with a smile at the beaux, who passing by turned their glasses up to her, and said: "She is a heavenly woman, the Hofräthinn Heerbrand."

TWELFTH VIGIL

How deeply did I feel, in the centre of my spirit, the blessedness of the Student Anselmus, who now, indissolubly united with his gentle Serpentina, has withdrawn to the mysterious land of wonders, recognized by him as the home towards which his bosom, filled with strange forecastings, had always longed.   But in vain was all my striving to set before you, favourable reader, those glories with which Anselmus is encompassed, or even in the faintest degree to shadow them to you in words.   Reluctantly I could not but acknowledge the feebleness of my every expression.   I felt myself enthralled amid the paltrinesses of everyday life; I sickened in tormenting dissatisfaction; I glided about like a dreamer; in brief, I fell into that condition of the Student Anselmus, which, in the Fourth Vigil, I endeavoured to set before you.   It grieved me to the heart, when I glanced over the Eleven Vigils, now happily accomplished, and thought that to insert the Twelfth, the keystone of the whole, would never be permitted me.   For whenever, in the night I set myself to complete the work, it was as if mischievous spirits (they might be relations, perhaps cousins-german, of the slain witch) held a polished glittering piece of metal before me, in which I beheld my own mean self, pale, drawn, and melancholic, like Registrator Heerbrand after his bout of punch.   Then I threw down my pen, and hastened to bed, that I might behold the happy Anselmus and the fair Serpentina at least in my dreams.   This had lasted for several days and nights, when at length quite unexpectedly I received a note from Archivarius Lindhorst, in which he wrote to me as follows:

Respected Sir,—It is well known to me that you have written down, in Eleven Vigils, the singular fortunes of my good son-in-law Anselmus, whilom student, now poet; and are at present cudgelling your brains very sore, that in the Twelfth and Last Vigil you may tell somewhat of his happy life in Atlantis, where he now lives with my daughter, on the pleasant freehold, which I possess in that country. Now, notwithstanding I much regret that hereby my own peculiar nature is unfolded to the reading world; seeing it may, in my office as Privy Archivarius, expose me to a thousand inconveniences; nay, in the Collegium even give rise to the question: How far a Salamander can justly, and with binding consequences, plight himself by oath, as a Servant of the State? and how far, on the whole, important affairs may be intrusted to him, since, according to Gabalis and Swedenborg, the spirits of the elements are not to be trusted at all?—notwithstanding, my best friends must now avoid my embrace; fearing lest, in some sudden anger, I dart out a flash or two, and singe their hair-curls, and Sunday frocks; notwithstanding all this, I say, it is still my purpose to assist you in the completion of the work, since much good of me and of my dear married daughter (would the other two were off my hands also!) has therein been said.

If you would write your Twelfth Vigil, descend your cursed five flights of stairs, leave your garret, and come over to me.   In the blue palmtree-room, which you already know, you will find fit writing materials; and you can then, in few words, specify to your readers, what you have seen; a better plan for you than any long-winded description of a life which you know only by hearsay. With esteem,

Your obedient servant,
The Salamander Lindhorst,
P. T. Royal Archivarius.

This somewhat rough, yet on the whole friendly note from Archivarius Lindhorst, gave me high pleasure. It seemed clear enough, indeed, that the singular manner in which the fortunes of his son-in-law had been revealed to me, and which I, bound to silence, must conceal even from you, gracious reader, was well known to this peculiar old gentleman; yet he had not taken it so ill as I might have apprehended. Nay, here was he offering me a helping hand in the completion of my work; and from this I might justly conclude, that at bottom he was not averse to having his marvellous existence in the world of spirits thus divulged through the press.

"It may be," thought I, "that he himself expects from this measure, perhaps, to get his two other daughters married sooner: for who knows but a spark may fall in this or that young man's breast, and kindle a longing for the green snake; whom, on Ascension Day, under the elder-bush, he will forthwith seek and find? From the misery which befell Anselmus, when he was enclosed in the glass bottle, he will take warning to be doubly and trebly on his guard against all doubt and unbelief."

Precisely at eleven o'clock, I extinguished my study lamp; and glided forth to Archivarius Lindhorst, who was already waiting for me in the lobby.

"Are you there, my worthy friend? Well, this is what I like, that you have not mistaken my good intentions: follow me!"

And with this he led the way through the garden, now filled with dazzling brightness, into the azure chamber, where I observed the same violet table, at which Anselmus had been writing.

Archivarius Lindhorst disappeared: but soon came back, carrying in his hand a fair golden goblet, out of which a high blue flame was sparkling up. "Here," said he, "I bring you the favourite drink of your friend the Bandmaster, Johannes Kreisler. It is burning arrack, into which I have thrown a little sugar. Sip a little of it: I will doff my dressing gown, and to amuse myself and enjoy your worthy company while you sit looking and writing, I shall just bob up and down a little in the goblet."

"As you please, honoured Herr Archivarius," answered I: "but if I am to ply the liquor, you will get none."

"Don't fear that, my good fellow," cried the Archivarius; then hastily throwing off his dressing gown, he mounted, to my no small amazement, into the goblet, and vanished in the blaze. Without fear, softly blowing back the flame, I partook of the drink: it was truly precious!

Stir not the emerald leaves of the palm-trees in soft sighing and rustling, as if kissed by the breath of the morning wind? Awakened from their sleep, they move, and mysteriously whisper of the wonders, which from the far distance approach like tones of melodious harps! The azure rolls from the walls, and floats like airy vapour to and fro; but dazzling beams shoot through it; and whirling and dancing, as in jubilee of childlike sport, it mounts and mounts to immeasurable height, and vaults over the palm-trees. But brighter and brighter shoots beam upon beam, till in boundless expanse the grove opens where I behold Anselmus. Here glowing hyacinths, and tulips, and roses, lift their fair heads; and their perfumes, in loveliest sound, call to the happy youth: "Wander, wander among us, our beloved; for you understand us! Our perfume is the longing of love: we love you, and are yours for evermore!" The golden rays burn in glowing tones: "We are fire, kindled by love. Perfume is longing; but fire is desire: and do we not dwell in your bosom? We are yours!" The dark bushes, the high trees rustle and sound: "Come to us, beloved, happy one! Fire is desire; but hope is our cool shadow. Lovingly we rustle round your head: for you understand us, because love dwells in your breast!" The brooks and fountains murmur and patter: "Loved one, do not walk so quickly by: look into our crystal! Your image dwells in us, which we preserve with love, for you have understood us." In the triumphal choir, bright birds are singing: "Hear us! Hear us! We are joy, we are delight, the rapture of love!" But anxiously Anselmus turns his eyes to the glorious temple, which rises behind him in the distance. The fair pillars seem trees; and the capitals and friezes acanthus leaves, which in wondrous wreaths and figures form splendid decorations. Anselmus walks to the Temple: he views with inward delight the variegated marble, the steps with their strange veins of moss. "Ah, no!" cries he, as if in the excess of rapture, "she is not far from me now; she is near!" Then Serpentina advances, in the fullness of beauty and grace, from the Temple; she bears the Golden Flower Pot, from which a bright lily

has sprung. The nameless rapture of infinite longing glows in her
meek eyes; she looks at Anselmus, and says: "Ah! Dearest, the Lily
has opened her blossom: what we longed for is fulfilled; is there a
happiness to equal ours?" Anselmus clasps her with the tenderness
of warmest ardour: the lily burns in flaming beams over his head.
And louder move the trees and bushes; clearer and gladder play
the brooks; the birds, the shining insects dance in the waves of
perfume: a gay, bright rejoicing tumult, in the air, in the water, in
the earth, is holding the festival of love! Now sparkling streaks
rush, gleaming over all the bushes; diamonds look from the ground
like shining eyes: strange vapours are wafted hither on sounding
wings: they are the spirits of the elements, who do homage to the
lily, and proclaim the happiness of Anselmus. Then Anselmus
raises his head, as if encircled with a beamy glory. Is it looks? Is
it words? Is it song? You hear the sound: "Serpentina! Belief
in you, love of you has unfolded to my soul the inmost spirit of
nature! You have brought me the lily, which sprang from gold,
from the primeval force of the world, before Phosphorus had kindled
the spark of thought; this lily is knowledge of the sacred harmony
of all beings; and in this I live in highest blessedness for evermore.
Yes, I, thrice happy, have perceived what was highest: I must
indeed love thee forever, O Serpentina! Never shall the golden
blossoms of the lily grow pale; for, like belief and love, this knowledge is eternal."

For the vision, in which I had now beheld Anselmus bodily, in
his freehold of Atlantis, I stand indebted to the arts of the Salamander; and it was fortunate that when everything had melted into
air, I found a paper lying on the violet-table, with the foregoing
statement of the matter, written fairly and distinctly by my own
hand. But now I felt myself as if transpierced and torn in pieces
by sharp sorrow. "Ah, happy Anselmus, who has cast away the
burden of everyday life, who in the love of kind Serpentina flies
with bold pinion, and now lives in rapture and joy on your freehold
in Atlantis! while I—poor I!—must soon, nay, in few moments,
leave even this fair hall, which itself is far from a Freehold in Atlantis;
and again be transplanted to my garret, where, enthralled among
the pettinesses of existence, my heart and my sight are so bedimmed
with thousand mischiefs, as with thick fog, that the fair lily will
never, never be beheld by me."

Then Archivarius Lindhorst patted me gently on the shoulder,
and said: "Softly, softly, my honoured friend! Do not lament so!

Were you not even now in Atlantis; and have you not at least a pretty little copyhold farm there, as the poetical possession of your inward sense?   And is the blessedness of Anselmus anything else but a living in poesy?   Can anything else but poesy reveal itself as the sacred harmony of all beings, as the deepest secret of nature?"

The Nutcracker

CHRISTMAS EVE

On the twenty-fourth of December, Dr. Stahlbaum's children were not allowed on any pretext whatever at any time that day to go into the small drawing-room, much less into the best drawing-room into which it opened. Fritz and Marie were sitting cowering together in a corner of the back parlour when the evening twilight fell, and they began to feel terribly eerie. Seeing that no candles were brought, as was generally the case on Christmas Eve, Fritz, whispering in a mysterious fashion, confided to his young sister (who was just seven) that he had heard rattlings and rustlings going on all day, since early morning, inside the forbidden rooms, as well as distant hammering. Further, that a short time ago a little dark-looking man had gone slipping and creeping across the floor with a big box under his arm, though he was well aware that this little man was no other than Godpapa Drosselmeier. At this news Marie clapped her little hands with joy, and cried:

"Oh! I do wonder what pretty things Godpapa Drosselmeier has been making for us *this* time!"

Godpapa Drosselmeier was anything but a nice-looking man. He was small and lean, with a great many wrinkles on his face, a big patch of black plaster where his right eye ought to have been, and not a hair on his head; which was why he wore a fine white wig, made of glass, and a very beautiful work of art. But he was a very, very clever man, who even knew and understood all about clocks and watches, and could make them himself. So that when one of the beautiful clocks that were in Dr. Stahlbaum's house was out of sorts and couldn't sing, Godpapa Drosselmeier would come, take off his glass periwig and his little yellow coat, gird himself with a blue apron, and proceed to stick sharp-pointed instruments into the inside of the clock in a way that made little Marie quite miserable to witness. However, this didn't really hurt the poor clock, which, on the contrary, would come to life again, and begin to whirr and sing and strike as merrily as ever; which caused everybody the greatest

satisfaction.   Of course, whenever he came he always brought
something delightful in his pockets for the children—perhaps a
little man, who would roll his eyes and make bows and scrapes, most
comic to behold; or a box, out of which a little bird would jump; or
something else of the kind.   But for Christmas he always had some
specially charming piece of ingenuity; something which had cost
him infinite pains and labour—for which reason it was always taken
away and put aside with the greatest care by the children's parents.

. "Oh! what can Godpapa Drosselmeier have been making for us
this time," Marie cried, as we have said.

Fritz was of the opinion that this time it could hardly be anything
but a great castle, a fortress, where all sorts of pretty soldiers would
be drilling and marching about; and then, that other soldiers would
come and try to get into the fortress, upon which the soldiers inside
would fire away at them, as pluckily as you please, with cannon, till
everything banged and thundered like anything.

"No, no," Marie said.   "Godpapa Drosselmeier once told me
about a beautiful garden with a great lake in it, and beautiful swans
swimming about with great gold collars, singing lovely music.
And then a lovely little girl comes down through the garden to the
lake, and calls the swans and feeds them with shortbread and cake."

"Swans don't eat cake and shortbread," Fritz cried, rather
rudely (with masculine superiority), "and Godpapa Drosselmeier
couldn't make a whole garden.   After all, we have got very few of
his playthings; whatever he brings is always taken away from us.
So I like the things papa and mamma give us much better; we
keep them, all right, ourselves, and can do what we like with
them."

The children went on discussing what he might have in store for
them this time.   Marie called Fritz's attention to the fact that Miss
Gertrude (her biggest doll) appeared to be failing a good deal as
time went on, inasmuch as she was more clumsy and awkward than
ever, tumbling on to the floor every two or three minutes.   This
did not occur without leaving very ugly marks on her face, and of
course proper condition of her clothes became out of the question
altogether.   Scolding was of no use.   Mamma too had laughed at
her for being so delighted with Miss Gertrude's little new parasol.
Fritz, again, remarked that a good fox was needed for his small
zoological collection, and that his army was quite without cavalry,
as his papa was well aware.   But the children knew that their
elders had got all sorts of charming things ready for them, and that
the Christ Child, at Christmas time, took special care for their

wants. Marie sat in thoughtful silence, but Fritz murmured quietly to himself:

"All the same, I should like a fox and some hussars!"

It was now quite dark. Fritz and Marie, sitting close together, did not dare to utter another syllable; they felt as if there were a fluttering of gentle, invisible wings around them, while a very distant, but unutterably beautiful strain of music could dimly be heard. Then a bright gleam of light passed quickly across the wall, and the children knew that the Christ Child had sped away on shining wings to other happy children. At this moment a silvery bell said, "Kling-ling! Kling-ling!" the doors flew open, and such a brilliance of light came streaming from the drawing-room that the children stood rooted where they were with cries of "Oh! Oh!"

Papa and mamma came and took their hands, saying, "Come now, darlings, and see what the blessed Christ Child has brought for you."

THE CHRISTMAS PRESENTS

I appeal to you, kind reader (or listener)—Fritz, Theodore, Ernest, or whatsoever your name may be—and I beg you to bring vividly before your mind's eye your last Christmas table, all glorious with its various delightful Christmas presents; and then perhaps you will be able to form some idea of the manner in which the two children stood speechless with their eyes fixed on all the beautiful things; how after a while, Marie, with a sigh, cried, "Oh, how lovely! how lovely!" and Fritz gave several jumps of delight.

The children had certainly been very, very good and well-behaved all the foregoing year to be thus rewarded; for never before had so many beautiful and delightful things been provided for them. The great Christmas tree on the table bore many apples of silver and gold, and all its branches were heavy with bud and blossom, consisting of sugar almonds, many-tinted bon-bons, and all sorts of things to eat. Perhaps the prettiest thing about this wonder-tree, however, was the fact that in all the recesses of its spreading branches hundreds of little tapers glittered like stars, inviting the children to pluck its flowers and fruit. Also, all around the tree on every side everything shone and glittered in the loveliest manner. Oh, how many beautiful things there were! Who, oh who, could describe them all? Marie gazed there at the most delicious dolls, and all kinds of toys, and (what was the prettiest thing of all) a little silk dress with many-tinted ribbons was hung upon a projecting branch so that she could admire it on all sides; which she accordingly did, crying out several times, "Oh! what a lovely, lovely, darling little dress! And I suppose, I do believe, I shall really be allowed to put it on!" Fritz, in the meantime, had had two or three trials of how his new fox (which he had found tied to the table) could gallop and now stated that he seemed a wildish sort of brute; but, no matter, he felt sure he would soon get him well in order; and he set to work to muster his new squadron of hussars, admirably equipped, in red and gold uniforms, with real silver swords, and mounted on such shining white horses that you would have thought they were of pure silver too.

When the children had sobered down a little, and were beginning upon the beautiful picture books (which were open, so that you could see all sorts of most beautiful flowers and people of every hue, to say nothing of lovely children playing, all as naturally represented as if they were really alive and could speak), there came another tinkling of a bell, to announce the display of Godpapa Drosselmeier's Christmas present, which was on another table, against the wall, concealed by a curtain. When this curtain was drawn, what did the children behold?

On a green lawn, bright with flowers, stood a lordly castle with a great many shining windows and golden towers. A chime of bells was going on inside it; doors and windows opened, and you saw very small but beautiful ladies and gentlemen with plumed hats, and long robes down to their heels walking up and down in the rooms of it. In the central hall, which seemed all in a blaze, there were quantities of little candles burning in silver chandeliers; children in little short doublets were dancing to the chimes of the bells. A gentleman in an emerald green mantle came to a window, made signs, and then disappeared inside again; also, even Godpapa Drosselmeier himself (but scarcely taller than papa's thumb) came now and then, and stood at the castle door, then went in again.

Fritz had been looking on with the rest at the beautiful castle and the people walking about and dancing in it, with his arms leant on the table; then he said:

"Godpapa Drosselmeier, let *me* go into your castle for a little while."

Drosselmeier answered that this could not possibly be done. In which he was right; for it was silly of Fritz to want to go into a castle which was not so tall as himself, golden towers and all. And Fritz saw that this was so.

After a short time, as the ladies and gentlemen kept on walking about just in the same fashion, the children dancing, and the emerald man looking out at the same window, and Godpapa Drosselmeier coming to the door, Fritz cried impatiently:

"Godpapa Drosselmeier, please come out at that other door!"

"That can't be done, dear Fritz," answered Drosselmeier.

"Well," resumed Fritz, "make that green man that looks out so often walk about with the others."

"And that can't be done, either," said his godpapa, once more.

"Make the children come down, then," said Fritz. "I want to see them nearer."

"Nonsense, nothing of that sort can be done," cried Drosselmeier with impatience. "The machinery must work as it's doing now; it can't be altered, you know."

"Oh," said Fritz, "it can't be done, eh? Very well, then, Godpapa Drosselmeier, I'll tell you what it is. If your little creatures in the castle there can only always do the same thing, they're not much worth, and I think precious little of them! No, give me my hussars. They've got to maneuver backwards and forwards just as I want them, and are not fastened up in a house."

With which he made off to the other table, and set his squadron of silver horse trotting here and there, wheeling and charging and slashing right and left to his heart's content. Marie had slipped away softly, too, for she was tired of the promenading and dancing of the puppets in the castle, though, kind and gentle as she was, she did not like to show it as her brother did. Drosselmeier, somewhat annoyed, said to the parents, "After all, an ingenious piece of mechanism like this is not a matter for children, who don't understand it; I shall put my castle back in its box again." But mother came to the rescue, and made him show her the clever machinery which moved the figures, Drosselmeier taking it all to pieces, putting it together again, and quite recovering his temper in the process. So that he gave the children all sorts of delightful brown men and women with golden faces, hands and legs, which were made of ginger cake, and with which they were greatly content.

MARIE'S PET AND PROTÉGÉ

But there was a reason why Marie found it against the grain to come away from the table where the Christmas presents were laid out; and this was, that she had just noticed something there which she had not observed at first. Fritz's hussars having taken ground to the right at some distance from the tree, in front of which they had previously been paraded, there became visible a most delicious little man, who was standing there quiet and unobtrusive, as if waiting patiently till it should be his turn to be noticed.

Objection, considerable objection, might, perhaps, have been taken to him on the score of his figure, for his body was rather too tall and stout for his legs, which were short and slight; moreover, his head was a good deal too large. But much of this was atoned for by the elegance of his costume, which showed him to be a person of taste and cultivation. He had on a very pretty violet hussar's jacket, knobs and braid all over, pantaloons of the same, and the loveliest little boots ever seen even on a hussar officer— fitting his little legs just as if they had been painted on them. It was funny, certainly, that dressed in this style as he was he had a little, rather absurd, short cloak on his shoulders, which looked almost as if it were made of wood, and on his head a cap like a miner's. But Marie remembered that Godpapa Drosselmeier often appeared in a terribly ugly morning jacket, and with a frightful-looking cap on his head, and yet was a very very darling godpapa.

As Marie kept looking at this little man, whom she had quite fallen in love with at first sight, she saw more and more clearly what a sweet nature and disposition were legible in his countenance. Those green eyes of his (which stuck, perhaps, a little more prominently out of his head than was quite desirable) beamed with kindliness and benevolence. It was one of his beauties, too, that his chin was set off with a well-kept beard of white cotton, as this drew attention to the smile which his bright red lips always expressed.

"Oh, papa, dear!" cried Marie at last, "whose is that most darling little man beside the tree?"

"Well," was the answer, "that little fellow is going to do plenty of good service for all of you; he's going to crack nuts for you, and he is to belong to Louise just as much as to you and Fritz." With which papa took him up from the table, and on his lifting the end of the wooden cloak, the little man opened his mouth wider and wider, displaying two rows of very white, sharp teeth. Marie, directed by her father, put a nut into his mouth, and—knack—he had bitten it in two, so that the shells fell down, and Marie got the kernel. So then it was explained to all that this charming little man belonged to the Nutcracker family, and was practicing the profession of his ancestors. "And," said papa, "as friend Nutcracker seems to have made such an impression on you, Marie, he shall be given over to your special care and charge, though, as I said, Louise and Fritz are to have the same right to his services as you."

Marie took him into her arms at once, and made him crack some more nuts; but she picked out all the smallest, so that he might not have to open his mouth so terribly wide, because that was not nice for him. Then sister Louise came, and he had to crack some nuts for her too, which duty he seemed very glad to perform, as he kept on smiling most courteously.

Meanwhile, Fritz was a little tired, after so much drill and maneuvering, so he joined his sisters, and laughed beyond measure at the funny little fellow, who (as Fritz wanted his share of the nuts) was passed from hand to hand, and was continually snapping his mouth open and shut. Fritz gave him all the biggest and hardest nuts he could find, but all at once there was a "crack—crack," and three teeth fell out of Nutcracker's mouth, and his lower jaw became loose and wobbly.

"Ah! my poor darling Nutcracker," Marie cried, and took him away from Fritz.

"A nice sort of chap he is!" said Fritz. "Calls himself a nutcracker, and can't give a decent bite—doesn't seem to know much about his business. Hand him over here, Marie! I'll keep him biting nuts if he drops all the rest of his teeth, and his jaw into the bargain. What's the good of a chap like him!"

"No, no," said Marie, in tears; "you shan't have him, my darling Nutcracker; see how he's looking at me so mournfully, and showing me his poor sore mouth. You're a hard-hearted creature! You beat your horses, and you've had one of your soldiers shot."

"Those things must be done," said Fritz, "and you don't understand anything about such matters. But Nutcracker's as much mine as yours, so hand him over!"

Marie began to cry bitterly, and quickly wrapped the wounded Nutcracker up in her little pocket handkerchief. Papa and mamma came with Drosselmeier, who took Fritz's part, to Marie's regret. But papa said, "I have put Nutcracker in Marie's special charge, and as he seems to have need just now of her care, she has full power over him, and nobody else has anything to say in the matter. And I'm surprised that Fritz should expect further service from a man wounded in the execution of his duty. As a good soldier, he ought to know better than that."

Fritz was much ashamed, and, troubling himself no further as to nuts or nutcrackers, crept off to the other side of the table, where his hussars (having established the necessary outposts and videttes) were bivouacking for the night. Marie got Nutcracker's lost teeth together, bound a pretty white ribbon, taken from her dress, about his poor chin, and then wrapped the poor little fellow, who was looking very pale and frightened, more tenderly and carefully than before in her handkerchief. Thus she held him, rocking him like a child in her arms, as she looked at the picture books. She grew quite angry (which was not usual with her) with Godpapa Drosselmeier because he laughed so, and kept asking how she could make such a fuss about an ugly little fellow like that. That odd and peculiar likeness to Drosselmeier, which had struck her when she saw Nutcracker at first, occurred to her mind again now, and she said, with much earnestness:

"Who knows, godpapa, if you were to be dressed the same as my darling Nutcracker, and had on the same shining boots—who knows whether you mightn't look almost as handsome as he does?"

Marie did not understand why papa and mamma laughed so heartily, nor why Godpapa Drosselmeier's nose got so red, nor why he did not join so much in the laughter as before. Probably there was some special reason for these things.

WONDERFUL EVENTS

We must now explain that in the sitting-room on the left hand as you go in there stands against the wall a high, glass-fronted cupboard, where all the children's Christmas presents are yearly put away to be kept. Louise, the elder sister, was still quite little when her father had this cupboard constructed by a very skillful workman, who had put in it such transparent panes of glass, and altogether made the whole affair so splendid, that the things, when inside it, looked almost more shining and lovely than when one had them actually in one's hands.

In the upper shelves, which were beyond the reach of Fritz and Marie, were stowed Godpapa Drosselmeier's works of art; immediately under them was the shelf for the picture books. Fritz and Marie were allowed to do what they liked with the two lower shelves, but it always came about that the lowest one of all was where Marie put her dolls, as their place of residence, while Fritz utilized the shelf above this as cantonments for his troops. So that on the evening about which we are speaking, Fritz had quartered his hussars in his—the upper—shelf of these two. Marie had put

Miss Gertrude rather in a corner, established her new doll in the well-appointed chamber there, with all its appropriate furniture, and invited herself to tea and cakes with her. This chamber was splendidly furnished, everything on a first-rate scale, and in good and admirable style, as I have already said. I don't know if you, my observant reader, have the satisfaction of possessing an equally well-appointed room for your dolls: a little beautifully-flowered sofa, a number of the most charming little chairs, a nice little tea-table, and, above all, a beautiful little white bed, where your pretty darlings of dolls go to sleep? All this was in a corner of the shelf, the walls of which, in this part, had beautiful little pictures hanging on them; and you may well imagine that, in such a delightful chamber as this, the new doll (whose name, as Marie had discovered, was Miss Clara) thought herself extremely comfortably settled, and remarkably well off.

It was getting very late, not so very far from midnight, indeed, before the children could tear themselves away from all these Yule-tide fascinations, and Godpapa Drosselmeier had been gone a considerable time. They remained riveted beside the glass cupboard, although their mother several times reminded them that it was long after bedtime. "Yes," said Fritz, "I know well enough that these poor fellows (meaning his hussars) are tired enough, and awfully anxious to turn in for the night, though as long as I'm here, not a man-jack of them dares to nod his head." With which he went off. But Marie earnestly begged for just a little while longer, saying she had such a number of things to see to, and promising that as soon as she had them all settled she would go to bed at once. Marie was a very good and reasonable child, and therefore her mother allowed her to remain a little longer with her toys; but lest she should be too much occupied with her new doll and the other playthings and would forget to put out the candles which were lighted all around on the wall sconces, she herself put all of them out, leaving merely the lamp which hung from the ceiling to give a soft and pleasant light. "Come to bed soon, Marie, or you'll never be up in time in the morning," cried her mother as she went away into the bedroom.

As soon as Marie was alone, she set rapidly to work to do what she wanted most to do, which, though she scarcely knew why, she somehow did not like to set about in her mother's presence. She had been holding Nutcracker, wrapped in the handkerchief, carefully in her arms all this time, and she now laid him softly down on the table, gently unrolled the handkerchief, and examined his wounds.

Nutcracker was very pale, but at the same time he was smiling with a melancholy and pathetic kindliness which went straight to Marie's heart.

"Oh, my darling little Nutcracker!" said she, very softly, "don't you be vexed because brother Fritz has hurt you so: he didn't mean it, you know; he's only a little bit hardened with his soldiering and that, but he's a good, nice boy, I assure you. I'll take the greatest care of you, and nurse you, till you're quite, quite better and happy again. And your teeth shall be put in again for you, and your shoulder set right. Godpapa Drosselmeier will see to that; he knows how to do things of that kind —"

Marie could not finish what she was going to say, because at the mention of Godpapa Drosselmeier, friend Nutcracker made a most horrible, ugly face. A sort of sharp green sparkle seemed to dart out of his eyes. This was only for an instant, however; and just as Marie was going to be terribly frightened, she found that she was looking at the very same nice, kindly face, with the pathetic smile which she had seen before, and she saw plainly that it was nothing but some draught of air making the lamp flicker that had seemed to produce the change.

"Well!" she said, "I certainly am a silly girl to be so easily frightened, and think that a wooden doll could make faces at me! But I'm too fond, really, of Nutcracker, because he's so funny, and so kind and nice; and so he must be taken the greatest care of, and properly nursed till he's well."

With which she took him in her arms again, approached the cupboard, and kneeling down beside it, said to her new doll:

"I'm going to ask a favour of you, Miss Clara—that you will give up your bed to this poor sick, wounded Nutcracker, and make yourself as comfortable as you can on the sofa here. Remember that you're well and strong yourself, or you wouldn't have such fat, red cheeks, and that there are very few dolls who have as comfortable a sofa as this to lie upon."

Miss Clara, in her Christmas full-dress, looked very grand and disdainful, and said not so much as "Boo!"

"Very well," said Marie, "why should I make such a fuss, and stand on any ceremony?"—took the bed and moved it forward; laid Nutcracker carefully and tenderly down on it; wrapped another pretty ribbon taken from her own dress about his hurt shoulder, and drew the bedclothes up to his nose.

"But he shan't stay with that nasty Clara," she said, and moved the bed, with Nutcracker in it, to the upper shelf, so that it was

placed near the village in which Fritz's hussars had their cantonments. She closed the cupboard, and was moving away to go to
bed, when—listen, children!—there began a low soft rustling and
rattling, and a sort of whispering noise, all round, in all directions,
from all quarters of the room—behind the stove, under the chairs,
behind the cupboards.

The clock on the wall "warned" louder and louder, but could
not strike. Marie looked at it, and saw that the big gilt owl which
was on the top of it had drooped its wings so that they covered the
whole of the clock, and had stretched its catlike head, with the
crooked beak, a long way forward. And the "warning" kept
growing louder and louder, with distinct words: "Clocks, clocks,
stop ticking. No sound, but cautious 'warning.' Mouse-King's
ears are fine. Prr-prr. Only sing poom, poom; sing the olden
song of doom! prr-prr; poom, poom. Bells go chime! Soon rings
out the fated time!" And then came "Poom! poom!" quite
hoarsely and smothered, twelve times.

Marie grew terribly frightened, and was going to rush away as
best she could, when she noticed that Godpapa Drosselmeier was
up on the top of the clock instead of the owl, with his yellow coattails
hanging down on both sides like wings. But she manned herself,
and called out in a loud voice of anguish:

"Godpapa! godpapa! what are you up there for? Come down
to me, and don't frighten me so terribly, you naughty, naughty
Godpapa Drosselmeier!"

But then there began a sort of wild kickering and squeaking,
everywhere, all about, and presently there was a sound as of running
and trotting, as of thousands of little feet behind the walls, and
thousands of little lights began to glitter out between the chinks of
the woodwork. But they were not lights; no, no! little glittering
eyes; and Marie became aware that, everywhere, mice were peeping
and squeezing themselves out through every chink. Presently they
were trotting and galloping in all directions over the room; orderly
bodies, continually increasing, of mice, forming themselves into
regular troops and squadrons, in good order, just as Fritz's soldiers
did when maneuvers were going on.

As Marie was not afraid of mice (as many children are), she
could not help being amused by this, and her first alarm had nearly
left her, when suddenly there came such a sharp and terrible piping
noise that the blood ran cold in her veins. Ah! what did she see
then? Well, truly, kind reader, I know that your heart is in the
right place, just as much as my friend Field Marshal Fritz's is, but

if you had seen what now came before Marie's eyes, you would have made a clean pair of heels of it; nay, I consider that you would have plumped into your bed, and drawn the blankets further over your head than necessity demanded.

But poor Marie hadn't it in her power to do any such thing, because right at her feet, as if impelled by some subterranean power, sand, and lime, and broken stone came bursting up, and then seven mouse-heads with seven shining crowns upon them rose through the floor, hissing and piping in a most horrible way. Quickly the body of the mouse which had these seven crowned heads forced its way up through the floor. This enormous creature shouted, with its seven heads, aloud to the assembled multitude, squeaking to them with all the seven mouths in full chorus. Then the entire army set itself in motion, and went trot, trot, right up to the cupboard—and, in fact, to Marie, who was standing beside it.

Marie's heart had been beating so with terror that she had thought it must jump out of her breast, and she must die. But now it seemed to her as if the blood in her veins stood still. Half-fainting, she leant backwards, and then there was a "klirr, klirr, prr," and a pane of the cupboard, broken by her elbow, fell in shivers to the floor. She felt for a moment a sharp, stinging pain in her arm, but this seemed to make her heart lighter; she heard no more of the queaking and piping. Everything was quiet; and though she didn't dare to look, she thought the noise of the breaking glass had frightened the mice back to their holes.

But what came to pass then? Right behind Marie a movement seemed to commence in the cupboard, and small, faint voices began to be heard, saying:

> Come, awake, measures take;
> Out to the fight, out to the fight;
> Shield the right, shield the right;
> Arm and away, this is the night.

And harmonica bells began ringing as prettily as you please.

"Oh! that's my little peal of bells!" cried Marie, and went nearer and looked in. Then she saw that there was bright light in the cupboard, and everything was busily in motion there; dolls and little figures of various kinds all running about together, and struggling with their little arms. At this point, Nutcracker rose from his bed, cast off the bedclothes, and sprang with both feet onto the floor (of the shelf), crying out at the top of his voice:

> Knack, knack, knack,
> Stupid mousey pack,

All their skulls we'll crack.
Mousey pack, knack, knack,
Mousey pack, crick and crack,
Cowardly lot of schnack!

And with this he drew his little sword, waved it in the air, and cried:

"Ye, my trusty vassals, brethren and friends, are ye ready to stand by me in this great battle?"

Immediately three scaramouches, one pantaloon, four chimney-sweeps, two zither-players, and a drummer cried, in eager accents:

"Yes, your highness; we will stand by you in loyal duty; we will follow you to death, victory, and the fray!" And they precipitated themselves after Nutcracker (who, in the excitement of the moment, had dared that perilous leap) to the bottom shelf. Now *they* might well dare this perilous leap, for not only had they got plenty of clothes on, of cloth and silk, but besides, there was not much in their insides except cotton and sawdust, so that they plumped down like little wool-sacks. But as for poor Nutcracker, he would certainly have broken his arms and legs; for, bethink you, it was nearly two feet from where he had stood to the shelf below, and his body was as fragile as if he had been made of elm-wood. Yes, Nutcracker would have broken his arms and legs, had not Miss Clara started up at the moment of his spring, and received the hero, drawn sword and all, in her tender arms.

"Oh! you dear, good Clara!" cried Marie, "how I did misunderstand you. I believe you were quite willing to let dear Nutcracker have your bed."

But Miss Clara now cried, as she pressed the young hero gently to her silken breast:

"Oh, my lord! go not into this battle and danger, sick and wounded as you are. See how your trusty vassals, clowns and pantaloon, chimney-sweeps, zithermen and drummer, are already arrayed below; and the puzzle-figures in my shelf here are in motion and preparing for the fray! Deign, oh my lord, to rest in these arms of mine, and contemplate your victory from a safe coign of vantage."

Thus spoke Clara. But Nutcracker behaved so impatiently, and kicked so with his legs, that Clara was obliged to put him down on the shelf in a hurry. However, he at once sank gracefully on one knee, and expressed himself as follows:

"Oh, lady! the kind protection and aid which you have afforded me will ever be present to my heart, in battle and in victory!"

On this, Clara bowed herself so as to be able to take hold of him by his arms, raised him gently up, quickly loosed her girdle, which was ornamented with many spangles, and would have placed it about his shoulders. But the little man swiftly drew himself two steps back, laid his hand upon his heart, and said, with much solemnity:

"Oh, lady! do not bestow this mark of your favour upon me; for—" He hesitated, gave a deep sigh, took the ribbon with which Marie had bound him from his shoulders, pressed it to his lips, put it on as a token, and, waving his glittering sword, sprang like a bird over the ledge of the cupboard down to the floor.

You will observe, kind reader, that Nutcracker, even before he really came to life, had felt and understood all Marie's goodness and regard, and that it was because of his gratitude and devotion to her that he would not take or even wear Miss Clara's ribbon, although it was exceedingly pretty and charming. This good, true-hearted Nutcracker preferred Marie's much commoner and less pretentious token.

But what is going to happen now? At the moment when Nutcracker sprang down, the squeaking and piping began again worse than ever. Alas! under the big table, the hordes of the mouse army had taken up a position, densely massed, under the command of the terrible mouse with the seven heads. So what is to be the result?

THE BATTLE

"Beat the *Generale*, trusty vassal-drummer!" cried Nutcracker, very loudly, and immediately the drummer began to roll his drum in the most splendid style, so that the windows of the glass cupboard rattled and resounded. Then there began a cracking and a clattering inside, and Marie saw all the lids of the boxes in which Fritz's army was quartered bursting open. The soldiers all came out and jumped down to the bottom shelf, where they formed up in good order. Nutcracker hurried up and down the ranks, speaking words of encouragement.

"There's not a dog of a trumpeter taking the trouble to sound a call!" he cried in a fury. Then he turned to the pantaloon (who was looking decidedly pale), and wobbling his long chin a good deal, said in a solemn tone:

"I know how brave and experienced you are, General! What is essential here is a rapid comprehension of the situation, and immediate utilization of the passing moment. I entrust you with the

command of the cavalry and artillery.   You can do without a horse;
your own legs are long, and you can gallop on them as fast as is
necessary.   Do your duty!"

Immediately Pantaloon put his long, lean fingers to his mouth,
and gave such a piercing crow that it rang as if a hundred little
trumpets had been sounding lustily.   Then there began a tramping
and a neighing in the cupboard; and Fritz's dragoons and cuirassiers
—but above all, the new glittering hussars—marched out, and then
came to a halt, drawn up on the floor.   They then marched past
Nutcracker by regiments, with *guidons* flying and bands playing.
After this they wheeled into line, and formed up at right angles to
the line of march.   Upon this, Fritz's artillery came rattling up,
and formed action front in advance of the halted cavalry.   Then it
went "boom-boom!" and Marie saw the sugar-plums doing terrible
execution amongst the thickly-massed mouse-battalions, which
were powdered quite white by them, and greatly put to shame.
But a battery of heavy guns, which had taken up a strong position
on mamma's footstool, was what did the greatest execution; and
"poom-poom-poom!" kept up a murderous fire of gingerbread
nuts into the enemy's ranks with most destructive effect, mowing
the mice down in great numbers.

The enemy, however, was not materially checked in his advance,
and had even possessed himself of one or two of the heavy guns,
when there came "prr-prr-prr!" and Marie could scarcely see what
was happening for smoke and dust; but this much is certain, that
every corps engaged fought with the utmost bravery and deter-
mination, and it was for a long time doubtful which side would gain
the day.   The mice kept on developing fresh bodies of their forces,
as they were advanced to the scene of action; their little silver balls
—like pills in size—which they delivered with great precision (their
musketry practice being especially fine) took effect even inside the
glass cupboard.   Clara and Gertrude ran up and down in utter
despair, wringing their hands, and loudly lamenting.

"Must I—the very loveliest doll in all the world—perish miser-
ably in the very flower of my youth?" cried Miss Clara.

"Oh! was it for this," wept Gertrude, "that I have taken such
pains to *conserver* myself all these years?   Must I be shot here in my
own drawing-room after all?"

On this, they fell into each other's arms, and howled so terribly
that you could hear them above all the din of the battle.   For you
have no idea of the hurly-burly that went on now, dear auditor!
It went prr-prr-poof, piff-schnetterdeng—schnetterdeng—boom-

booroom—boom-booroom—boom—all confusedly and higgledy-piggledy; and the mouse-king and the mice squeaked and screamed; and then again Nutcracker's powerful voice was heard shouting words of command, and issuing important orders, and he was seen striding along amongst his battalions in the thick of the fire.

Pantaloon had made several most brilliant cavalry charges, and covered himself with glory. But Fritz's hussars were subjected—by the mice—to a heavy fire of very evil-smelling shot, which made horrid spots on their red tunics; this caused them to hesitate, and hang rather back for a time. Pantaloon made them take ground to the left, in échelon, and in the excitement of the moment he, with his dragoons and cuirassiers, executed a somewhat analogous move-ment. That is to say, they brought up the right shoulder, wheeled to the left, and marched home to their quarters. This had the effect of bringing the battery of artillery on the footstool into imminent danger, and it was not long before a large body of exceedingly ugly mice delivered such a vigorous assault on this position that the whole of the footstool, with the guns and gunners, fell into the enemy's hands.

Nutcracker seemed much disconcerted, and ordered his right wing to commence a retrograde movement. A soldier of your experience, my dear Fritz, knows well that such a movement is almost tantamount to a regular retreat, and you grieve with me in anticipation, for the disaster which threatens the army of Marie's beloved little Nut-cracker. But turn your glance in the other direction, and look at this left wing of Nutcracker's, where all is still going well, and you will see that there is still much hope for the commander-in-chief and his cause.

During the hottest part of the engagement, masses of mouse cavalry had been quietly debouching from under the chest of drawers, and had subsequently made a most determined advance upon the left wing of Nutcracker's force, uttering loud and horrible squeakings. But what a reception they met with! Very slowly, as the nature of the terrain necessitated (for the ledge at the bottom of the cupboard had to be passed), the regiment of motto figures, commanded by two Chinese Emperors, advanced, and formed a square. These fine, brilliantly uniformed troops, consisting of gardeners, Tyrolese, Tungooses, hairdressers, harlequins, Cupids, lions, tigers, unicorns, and monkeys, fought with the utmost courage, coolness, and steady endurance.

This *bataillon d'élite* would have wrested the victory from the enemy had not one of the mouse cavalry captains, pushing forward in a rash and foolhardy manner, made a charge upon one of the Chinese Emperors and bitten off his head. This Chinese Emperor, in his fall, knocked over and smothered a couple of Tungooses and a unicorn, and this created a gap through which the enemy effected a rush, which resulted in the whole battalion being bitten to death. But the enemy gained little advantage by this; for as soon as one of the mouse-cavalry soldiers bit one of these brave adversaries to death, he found that there was a small piece of printed paper sticking in his throat, of which he died in a moment. Still, this was of small advantage to Nutcracker's army, which, having once commenced a retrograde movement, went on retreating farther and farther, suffering greater and greater loss. The unfortunate Nutcracker soon found himself driven back close to the front of the cupboard, with a very small remnant of his army.

"Bring up the reserves! Pantaloon! Scaramouch! Drummer! where the devil have you got to?" shouted Nutcracker, who was still reckoning on reinforcements from the cupboard. And there did, in fact, advance a small contingent of brown gingerbread men and women, with gilt faces, hats, and helmets; but they laid about them so clumsily that they never hit any of the enemy, and soon knocked off the cap of their commander-in-chief, Nutcracker himself. And the enemy's chasseurs soon bit their legs off, so that they tumbled topsy-turvy, and killed several of Nutcracker's companions-in-arms into the bargain.

Nutcracker was now hard pressed, and closely hemmed in by the enemy, and in a position of extreme peril. He tried to jump the bottom ledge of the cupboard, but his legs were not long enough. Clara and Gertrude had fainted; so they could give him no assistance. Hussars and heavy dragoons came charging up at him, and he shouted in wild despair:

"A horse! a horse! My kingdom for a horse!"

At this moment two of the enemy's riflemen seized him by his wooden cloak, and the king of the mice went rushing up to him, squeaking in triumph out of all his seven throats.

Marie could contain herself no longer. "Oh! my poor Nutcracker!" she sobbed, took her left shoe off, without very distinctly knowing what she was about, and threw it as hard as she could into the thick of the enemy, straight at their king.

Instantly everything vanished and disappeared. All was silence. Nothing was to be seen. But Marie felt a more stinging pain than before in her left arm, and fell on the floor insensible.

THE INVALID

When Marie awoke from a deathlike sleep she was lying in her little bed; and the sun was shining brightly in at the window, which was all covered with frost-flowers. There was a strange gentleman sitting beside her, whom she recognized as Dr. Wendelstern. "She's awake," he said softly, and her mother came and looked at her very scrutinizingly and anxiously.

"Oh, mother!" whispered Marie, "are all those horrid mice gone away, and is Nutcracker quite safe?"

"Don't talk such nonsense, Marie," answered her mother. "What have the mice to do with Nutcracker? You're a very naughty girl, and have caused us all a great deal of anxiety. See what comes of children not doing as they're told! You were playing with your toys so late last night that you fell asleep. I don't know whether or not some mouse jumped out and frightened you, though there are no mice here, generally. But you broke a pane of the glass cupboard with your elbow, and cut your arm so badly that Dr. Wendelstern (who has just taken a number of pieces of the glass out of your arm) thinks that if it had been a little higher up you might have had a stiff arm for life, or even have bled to death. Thank Heaven, I awoke about twelve o'clock and missed you; and I found you lying insensible in front of the glass cupboard, bleeding frightfully, with a number of Fritz's lead soldiers scattered round you, and other toys, broken motto figures, and gingerbread men; and Nutcracker was lying on your bleeding arm, with your left shoe not far off."

"Oh, mother, mother," said Marie, "these were the remains of the tremendous battle between the toys and the mice; and what frightened me so terribly was that the mice were going to take Nutcracker (who was the commander-in-chief of the toy army) prisoner. Then I threw my shoe in among the mice, and after that I know nothing more that happened."

Dr. Wendelstern gave a significant look at the mother, who said very gently to Marie:

"Never mind, dear, keep yourself quiet. The mice are all gone away, and Nutcracker's in the cupboard, quite safe and sound."

Here Marie's father came in, and had a long consultation with Dr. Wendelstern. Then he felt Marie's pulse, and she heard them talking about "wound-fever." She had to stay in bed and take medicine for some days, although she didn't feel at all ill, except that her arm was rather stiff and painful. She knew Nutcracker had got safe out of the battle, and she seemed to remember, as if in

a dream, that he had said, quite distinctly, in a very melancholy
tone:

"Marie! dearest lady! I am most deeply indebted to you. But
it is in your power to do even more for me."

She thought and thought what this could possibly be, but in vain;
she couldn't make it out. She wasn't able to play on account of her
arm; and when she tried to read, or look through the picture books,
everything wavered before her eyes so strangely that she was obliged
to stop. The days seemed very long to her, and she could scarcely
pass the time till evening, when her mother came and sat at her bedside, telling and reading her all sorts of nice stories. She had just
finished telling her the story of Prince Fakardin, when the door
opened and in came Godpapa Drosselmeier, saying:

"I've come to see with my own eyes how Marie's getting on."

When Marie saw Godpapa Drosselmeier in his little yellow coat,
the scene of the night when Nutcracker lost the battle with the mice
came so vividly back to her that she couldn't help crying out:

"Oh! Godpapa Drosselmeier, how nasty you were! I saw you
quite well when you were sitting on the clock, covering it all over
with your wings to prevent it from striking and frightening the mice.
I heard you quite well when you called the Mouse-King. Why
didn't you help Nutcracker? Why didn't you help *me*, you nasty
god-papa? It's nobody's fault but yours that I'm lying here with
a bad arm."

Her mother, in much alarm, asked what she meant. But
Drosselmeier began making extraordinary faces, and said, in a
snarling voice, like a sort of chant in monotone:

"Pendulums could only rattle—couldn't tick, ne'er a click; all
the clocks stopped their ticking: no more clicking; then they all
struck loud, cling-clang. Dolls! Don't your heads hang down!
Hink and hank, and honk and hank. Doll-girls! don't hang your
heads! Cling and ring! The battle's over—Nutcracker all safe
in clover. Comes the owl, on downy wing—Scares away the
mouses' king. Pak and pik and pik and pook—clocks, bim-boom—
grr-grr. Pendulums must click again. Tick and tack, grr and brr,
prr and purr."

Marie fixed wide eyes of terror upon Godpapa Drosselmeier,
because he was looking quite different and far more horrid than
usual, and was jerking his right arm backwards and forwards as if
he were some puppet moved by a handle. She was beginning to
grow terribly frightened at him when her mother came in, and Fritz
(who had arrived in the meantime) laughed heartily, crying, "Why,

godpapa, you *are* going on funnily!   You're just like my old Jumping Jack that I threw away last month."

But the mother looked very grave, and said, "This is a most extraordinary way of going on, Mr. Drosselmeier.   What can you mean by it?"

"My goodness!" said Drosselmeier, laughing, "did you never hear my nice Watchmaker's Song?   I always sing it to little invalids like Marie."   Then he hastened to sit down beside Marie's bed, and said to her, "Don't be vexed with me because I didn't gouge out all the Mouse-King's fourteen eyes.   That couldn't be managed exactly; but to make up for it, here's something which I know will please you greatly."

He dived into one of his pockets, and what he slowly, slowly brought out of it was—Nutcracker! whose teeth he had put in again quite firmly, and set his broken jaw completely to rights.   Marie shouted for joy, and her mother laughed and said, "Now you see for yourself how nice Godpapa Drosselmeier is to Nutcracker."

"But you must admit, Marie," said her godpapa, "that Nutcracker is far from being what you might call a handsome fellow, and you can't say he has a pretty face.   If you like, I'll tell you how it was that the ugliness came into his family, and has been handed down in it from one generation to another.   Did ever you hear about the Princess Pirlipat, the witch Mouserink, and the clever Clockmaker?"

"I say, Godpapa Drosselmeier," interrupted Fritz at this juncture, "you've put Nutcracker's teeth in again all right, and his jaw isn't wobbly as it was; but what's become of his sword?   Why haven't you given him a sword?"

"Oh," cried Drosselmeier, annoyed, "you must always be bothering and finding fault with something or other, boy.   What have I to do with Nutcracker's sword?   I've put his mouth to rights for him; he must look out for a sword for himself."

"Yes, yes," said Fritz, "so he must, of course, if he's a right sort of fellow."

"So tell me, Marie," continued Drosselmeier, "if you know the story of Princess Pirlipat?"

"Oh no," said Marie.   "Tell it me, please—do tell it me!"

"I hope it won't be as strange and terrible as your stories generally are," said her mother.

"Oh no, nothing of the kind," said Drosselmeier.   "On the contrary, it's quite a funny story which I'm going to have the honour of telling this time."

"Go on then—do tell it to us," cried the children; and Drosselmeier commenced as follows:—

THE STORY OF THE HARD NUT

Pirlipat's mother was a king's wife, so that, of course, she was a queen; and Pirlipat herself was a princess by birth as soon as ever she was born. The king was quite beside himself with joy over his beautiful little daughter as she lay in her cradle, and he danced round and round upon one leg, crying again and again.

"Hurrah! hurrah! hip, hip, hurrah! Did anybody ever see anything so lovely as my little Pirlipat?"

And all the ministers of state, and the generals, the presidents, and the officers of the staff, danced about on one leg, as the king did, and cried as loud as they could, "No, no—never!"

Indeed, there was no denying that a lovelier baby than Princess Pirlipat was never born since the world began. Her little face looked as if it were woven of the most delicate white and rose-coloured silk; her eyes were of sparkling azure, and her hair all in little curls like threads of gold. Moreover, she had come into the world with two rows of little pearly teeth, with which, two hours after her birth, she bit the Lord High Chancellor in the fingers when he was making a careful examination of her features, so that he cried, "Oh! Gemini!" quite loudly.

There are persons who assert that "Oh Lord" was the expression he employed, and opinions are still considerably divided on this point. At all events, she bit him in the fingers; and the realm learned, with much gratification, that both intelligence and discrimination dwelt within her angelical little frame.

All was joy and gladness, as I have said, save that the queen was very anxious and uneasy, nobody could tell why. One remarkable circumstance was that she had Pirlipat's cradle most scrupulously guarded. Not only were there always guards at the doors of the nursery, but—over and above the two head nurses close to the cradle —there always had to be six other nurses all around the room at night. And what seemed rather a funny thing, which nobody could understand, was that each of these six nurses always had to have a cat in her lap, and to keep on stroking it all night long, so that it would never stop purring.

It is impossible that you, my reader, should know the reason of all these precautions; but I do, and shall proceed to tell you at once.

Once upon a time, many great kings and very grand princes were
assembled at Pirlipat's father's court, and very great doings were
afoot.   Tournaments, theatricals, and state balls were going on on
the grandest scale, and the king, to show that he had no lack of gold
and silver, made up his mind to make a good hole in the crown
revenues for once, and launch out regardless of expense.   Wherefore (having previously ascertained privately from the state head
master cook that the court astronomer had indicated a propitious
hour for pork-butchering), he resolved to give a grand pudding-and-
sausage banquet.   He jumped into a state carriage, and personally
invited all the kings and the princes—to a basin of soup, merely—
that he might enjoy their astonishment at the magnificence of
the entertainment.   Then he said to the queen, very graciously,
"My darling, *you* know exactly how I like my puddings and
sausages!"

The queen quite understood what this meant.   It meant that
she should undertake the important duty of making the puddings
and the sausages herself, which was a thing she had done on one or
two previous occasions.   So the chancellor of the exchequer was
ordered to issue out of store the great golden sausage kettle, and the
silver casseroles.   A great fire of sandalwood was kindled, the queen
put on her damask kitchen apron, and soon the most delicious aroma
of pudding broth rose steaming out of the kettle.   This sweet smell
penetrated into the very council chamber.   The king could not
control himself.

"Excuse me for a few minutes, my lords and gentlemen," he
cried, rushed to the kitchen, embraced the queen, stirred in the
kettle a little with his golden sceptre, and then went back easier in
his mind to the council chamber.

The important moment had now arrived when the fat had to be
cut up into little square pieces, and browned on silver spits.   The
ladies-in-waiting retired, because the queen, from motives of love
and duty to her royal consort, thought it proper to perform this
important task in solitude.   But when the fat began to brown, a
delicate little whispering voice made itself audible, saying, "Give
me some of that, sister!   I want some of it, too; I am a queen as
well as yourself; give me some."

The queen knew well who was speaking.   It was Dame Mouserink, who had been established in the palace for many years.   She
claimed relationship to the royal family, and she was queen of the
realm of Mousolia herself, and lived with a considerable retinue of
her own under the kitchen hearth.   The queen was a kind-hearted,

benevolent woman; and, although she didn't exactly care to recognize Dame Mouserink as a sister and a queen, she was willing, at this festive season, to spare her the tidbits she had a mind to. So she said, "Come out, then, Dame Mouserink; of course you shall taste my browned fat."

So Dame Mouserink came running out as fast as she could, held up her pretty little paws, and took morsel after morsel of the browned fat as the queen held them out to her. But then all Dame Mouserink's uncles, and her cousins, and her aunts, came jumping out too; and her seven sons (who were terrible ne'er-do-wells) into the bargain; and they all set to at the browned fat, and the queen was too frightened to keep them at bay. Most fortunately the mistress of the robes came in, and drove these importunate visitors away, so that a little of the browned fat was left; and then, when the court mathematician (an ex-senior wrangler of his university) was called in (which he had to be, on purpose), it was found possible, by means of skillfully devised apparatus provided with special micrometer screws, and so forth, to apportion and distribute the fat among the whole of the sausages, etc., under construction.

The kettledrums and the trumpets summoned all the great princes and potentates to the feast. They assembled in their robes of state; some of them on white palfreys, some in crystal coaches. The king received them with much gracious ceremony, and took his seat at the head of the table, with his crown on, and his sceptre in his hand. Even during the serving of the white pudding course, it was observed that he turned pale, and raised his eyes to heaven; sighs heaved his bosom; some terrible inward pain was clearly raging within him. But when the black puddings were handed round, he fell back in his seat, loudly sobbing and groaning.

Everyone rose from the table, and the court physician tried in vain to feel his pulse. Ultimately, after the administration of most powerful remedies—burnt feathers, and the like—His Majesty seemed to recover his senses to some extent, and stammered, scarce audibly, the words: "Too little fat!"

The queen cast herself down at his feet in despair, and cried, in a voice broken by sobs, "Oh, my poor unfortunate royal consort! Ah, what tortures you are doomed to endure! But see the culprit here at your feet. Punish her severely! Alas! Dame Mouserink, her uncles, her seven sons, her cousins and her aunts, came and ate up nearly all the fat—and—"

Here the queen fell back insensible.

But the king jumped up, all anger, and cried in a terrible voice, "Mistress of the robes, what is the meaning of this?"

The mistress of the robes told all she knew, and the king resolved to take revenge on Dame Mouserink and her family for eating up the fat which ought to have been in the sausages. The privy council was summoned, and it was resolved that Dame Mouserink should be tried for her life, and all her property confiscated. But as His Majesty was of opinion that she might go on consuming the fat, which was his appanage, the whole matter was referred to the court Clockmaker and Arcanist—whose name was the same as mine—Christian Elias Drosselmeier, and he undertook to expel Dame Mouserink and all her relations from the palace precincts forever, by means of a certain politico-diplomatic procedure. He invented certain ingenious little machines, into which pieces of browned fat were inserted; and he placed these machines down all about the dwelling of Dame Mouserink. Now she herself was much too knowing not to see through Drosselmeier's artifice; but all her remonstrances and warnings to her relations were unavailing. Enticed by the fragrant odour of the browned fat, all her seven sons, and a great many of her uncles, cousins and aunts, walked into Drosselmeier's little machines and were immediately taken prisoners by the fall of a small grating, after which they met with a shameful death in the kitchen.

Dame Mouserink left this scene of horror with her small following. Rage and despair filled her breast. The court rejoiced greatly; the queen was very anxious, because she knew Dame Mouserink's character, and knew well that she would never allow the death of her sons and other relatives to go unavenged. And, in fact, one day when the queen was cooking a fricassée of sheep's lights for the king (a dish to which he was exceedingly partial), Dame Mouserink suddenly made her appearance, and said: "My sons and my uncles, my cousins and my aunts, are now no more. Have a care, lady, lest the queen of the mice bites your little princess in two! Have a care!"

With which she vanished, and was no more seen. But the queen was so frightened that she dropped the fricassée into the fire; so this was the second time Dame Mouserink spoiled one of the king's favorite dishes, at which he was very irate.

But this is enough for tonight; we'll go on with the rest of it another time—said Drosselmeier.

Sorely as Marie—who had ideas of her own about this story—begged Godpapa Drosselmeier to go on with it, he would not be persuaded, but jumped up, saying, "Too much at a time wouldn't be good for you; the rest tomorrow."

Just as Drosselmeier was going out of the door, Fritz said: "I say, Godpapa Drosselmeier, was it really you who invented mousetraps?"

"How can you ask such silly questions?" cried his mother. But Drosselmeier laughed oddly, and said, "Well, you know I'm a clever clockmaker. Mousetraps had to be invented some time or other."

And now you know, children, said Godpapa Drosselmeier the next evening, why it was the queen took such precautions about her little Pirlipat. Had she not always the fear before her eyes of Dame Mouserink coming back and carrying out her threat of biting the princess to death? Drosselmeier's ingenious machines were of no avail against the clever, crafty Dame Mouserink, and nobody save the court astronomer, who was also state astrologer and reader of the stars, knew that the family of the Cat Purr had the power to keep her at bay. This was the reason why each of the lady nurses was obliged to keep one of the sons of that family (each of whom was given the honorary rank and title of "privy councillor of legation") in her lap, and render his onerous duty less irksome by gently scratching his back.

One night, just after midnight, one of the chief nurses stationed close to the cradle, woke suddenly from a profound sleep. Everything lay buried in slumber. Not a purr to be heard—deep, death-like silence, so that the death-watch ticking in the wainscot sounded quite loud. What were the feelings of this principal nurse when she saw, close beside her, a great, hideous mouse, standing on its hind legs, with its horrid head laid on the princess's face! She sprang up with a scream of terror. Everybody awoke; but then Dame Mouserink (for she was the great big mouse in Pirlipat's cradle) ran quickly away into the corner of the room. The privy councillors of legation dashed after her, but too late! She was off and away through a chink in the floor. The noise awoke Pirlipat, who cried terribly. "Heaven be thanked, she is still alive!" cried all the nurses; but what was their horror when they looked at Pirlipat, and saw what the beautiful, delicate little thing had turned into. An enormous bloated head (instead of the pretty little golden-haired one) at the top of a diminutive, crumpled-up body, and green, wooden-looking eyes staring where the lovely azure-blue pair had been, whilst her mouth had stretched across from the one ear to the other.

Of course the queen nearly died of weeping and loud lamentation, and the walls of the king's study had all to be hung with padded arras, because he kept on banging his head against them, crying:

"Oh! wretched king that I am! Oh, wretched king that I am!"

Of course he might have seen then, that it would have been much better to eat his puddings with no fat in them at all, and let Dame Mouserink and her folk stay on under the hearthstone. But Pirlipat's royal father did not think of that. What he did was to lay all the blame on the court Clockmaker and Arcanist, Christian Elias Drosselmeier, of Nuremberg. Wherefore he promulgated a sapient edict to the effect that said Drosselmeier should within the space of four weeks restore Princess Pirlipat to her pristine condition—or, at least, indicate an unmistakable and reliable process whereby that might be accomplished—or else suffer a shameful death by the axe of the common headsman.

Drosselmeier was not a little alarmed; but he soon began to place confidence in his art, and in his luck; so he proceeded to execute the first operation which seemed to him to be expedient. He took Princess Pirlipat very carefully to pieces, screwed off her hands and feet, and examined her interior structure. Unfortunately, he found that the bigger she got the more deformed she would be, so that he didn't see what was to be done at all. He put her carefully together again, and sank down beside her cradle—which he wasn't allowed to go away from—in the deepest dejection.

The fourth week had come, and Wednesday of the fourth week, when the king came in with eyes gleaming with anger, made threatening gestures with his sceptre, and cried:

"Christian Elias Drosselmeier, restore the princess, or prepare for death!"

Drosselmeier began to weep bitterly. The little princess kept on cracking nuts, an occupation which seemed to afford her much quiet satisfaction. For the first time the Arcanist was struck by Pirlipat's remarkable appetite for nuts, and the circumstance that she had been born with teeth. And the fact had been that immediately after her transformation she had begun to cry, and she had gone on crying till by chance she got hold of a nut. She at once cracked it, and ate the kernel, after which she was quite quiet. From that time her nurses found that nothing would do but to go on giving her nuts.

"Oh, holy instinct of nature—eternal, mysterious, inscrutable Interdependence of Things!" cried Drosselmeier, "thou pointest out to me the door of the secret. I will knock, and it shall be opened unto me."

He at once begged for an interview with the Court Astronomer, and was conducted to him closely guarded. They embraced with many tears for they were great friends, and then retired into a private closet, where they referred to many books treating of sympathies, antipathies, and other mysterious subjects. Night came on. The Court Astronomer consulted the stars, and with the assistance of Drosselmeier (himself an adept in astrology) drew the princess's horoscope. This was an exceedingly difficult operation, for the lines kept getting more and more entangled and confused for ever so long. But at last—oh what joy!—it lay plain before them that all the princess had to do to be delivered from the enchantment which made her so hideous and get back her former beauty was to eat the sweet kernel of the nut Crackatook.

Now this nut Crackatook had a shell so hard that you might have fired a forty-eight pounder at it without producing the slightest effect on it. Moreover, it was essential that this nut should be cracked, in the princess's presence, by the teeth of a man whose beard had never known a razor, and who had never had on boots. This man had to hand the kernel to her with his eyes closed, and he might not open them till he had made seven steps backwards without a stumble.

Drosselmeier and the astronomer had been at work on this problem uninterruptedly for three days and three nights; and on the Saturday the king was sitting at dinner when Drosselmeier—who was to have been beheaded on the Sunday morning—burst in joyfully to announce that he had found out what had to be done to restore Princess Pirlipat to her pristine beauty. The king embraced him in a burst of rapture, and promised him a diamond sword, four decorations, and two Sunday suits.

"Set to work immediately after dinner," the monarch cried, adding kindly, "Take care, dear Arcanist, that the young unshaven gentleman in shoes, with the nut Crackatook all ready in his hand, is on the spot; and be sure that he touches no liquor beforehand, so that he mayn't trip up when he makes his seven backward steps like a crab. He can get as drunk as a lord afterwards, if he likes."

Drosselmeier was dismayed at this utterance of the king's, and stammered out, not without trembling and hesitation, that, though the remedy was discovered, both the nut Crackatook and the young gentleman who was to crack it had still to be searched for, and that it was matter of doubt whether they ever would be found at all.

The king, greatly incensed, whirled his sceptre round his crowned head, and shouted in the voice of a lion:

"Very well, then you must be beheaded!"

It was exceedingly fortunate for the wretched Drosselmeier that the king had thoroughly enjoyed his dinner that day, and was consequently in an admirable temper, and disposed to listen to the sensible advice which the queen, who was very sorry for Drosselmeier, did not hesitate to give him. Drosselmeier took heart and represented that he really had fulfilled the conditions, discovered the necessary measures, and gained his life, consequently. The king said this was all bosh and nonsense; but at length, after two or three glasses of liqueurs decreed that Drosselmeier and the astronomer should start off immediately, and not come back without the nut Crackatook in their pockets. The man who was to crack it (by the queen's suggestion) might be heard of by means of advertisements in the local and foreign newspapers and gazettes.

Godpapa Drosselmeier interrupted his story at this point, and promised to finish it on the following evening.

Next evening, as soon as the lights were brought, Godpapa Drosselmeier duly arrived, and went on with his story as follows:—

Drosselmeier and the court astronomer had been journeying for fifteen long years without finding the slightest trace of the nut Crackatook. I might go on for more than four weeks telling you where all they had been and what extraordinary things they had seen. I shall not do so, however, but merely mention that Drosselmeier in his profound discouragement at last began to feel a most powerful longing to see his dear native town of Nuremberg once again. And he was more powerfully moved by this longing than usual one day, when he happened to be smoking a pipe of kanaster with his friend in the middle of a great forest in Asia, and he cried:

"Oh, Nuremberg, Nuremberg, dear native town—he who still knows thee not, place of renown—though far he has travelled, and great cities seen—as London, and Paris, and Peterwardein—knoweth not what it is happy to be—still must his longing heart languish for thee—for thee, O Nuremberg, exquisite town—where the houses have windows both upstairs and down!"

As Drosselmeier lamented dolefully, the astronomer, seized with compassionate sympathy, began to weep and howl so terribly that he was heard throughout the length and breadth of Asia. But he collected himself again, wiped the tears from his eyes, and said:

"After all, dearest colleague, why should we sit and weep and howl here? Why not go to Nuremberg? Does it matter a brass farthing, after all, where and how we search for this horrible nut Crackatook?"

"That's true, too," answered Drosselmeier, consoled. They both got up immediately, knocked the ashes out of their pipes, started off, and travelled straight on without stopping from that forest right in the centre of Asia till they came to Nuremberg. As soon as they got there, Drosselmeier went straight to his cousin the toymaker and doll-carver, and gilder and varnisher, whom he had not seen for a great many long years. To him he told all the tale of Princess Pirlipat, Dame Mouserink, and the nut Crackatook, so that he clapped his hands repeatedly and cried in amazement:

"Dear me, cousin, these things are really wonderful—very wonderful, indeed!"

Drosselmeier told him, further, some of the adventures he had met with on his long journey—how he had spent two years at the court of the King of Dates; how the Prince of Almonds had expelled him with ignominy from his territory; how he had applied in vain to the Natural History Society at Squirreltown—in short, how he had been everywhere utterly unsuccessful in discovering the faintest trace of the nut Crackatook. During this narrative, Christoph Zacharias had kept frequently snapping his fingers, twisting himself round on one foot, smacking with his tongue, etc.; then he cried:

"Ey—aye—oh!—that really would be the very deuce and all."

At last he threw his hat and wig in the air, warmly embraced his cousin, and cried:

"Cousin, cousin, you're a made man—a made man you are—for either I am much deceived, or I have the nut Crackatook myself!"

He immediately produced a little cardboard box, out of which he took a gilded nut of medium size.

"Look there!" he said, showing this nut to his cousin; "the state of matters as regards this nut is this. Several years ago at Christmas time a stranger came here with a sack of nuts, which he offered for sale. Just in front of my shop he got into a quarrel, and put the sack down the better to defend himself from the nutsellers of the place, who attacked him. Just then a heavily loaded wagon drove over the sack, and all the nuts were smashed but one. The stranger, with an odd smile, offered to sell me this nut for a twenty-kreuzer piece of the year 1796. This struck me as strange. I found just such a coin in my pocket, so I bought the nut, and I gilt it, though I didn't know why I took the trouble, or should have given so much for it."

All question as to its being really the long-sought nut Crackatook was dispelled when the Court Astronomer carefully scraped away the gilding, and found the word "Crackatook" graven on the shell in Chinese characters.

The joy of the exiles was great, as you may imagine; and the cousin was even happier, for Drosselmeier assured him that *he* was a made man too, as he was sure of a good pension, and all the gold leaf he would want for the rest of his life for his gilding, free, gratis, for nothing.

The Arcanist and the Astronomer both had on their nightcaps, and were going to turn into bed, when the astronomer said:

"I tell you what it is, my dear colleague, one piece of good fortune never comes alone. I feel convinced that we've not only found the nut, but the young gentleman who is to crack it, and hand the beauty-restoring kernel to the princess, into the bargain. I mean none other than your cousin's son here, and I don't intend to close an eye this night till I've drawn that youngster's horoscope."

With which he threw away his nightcap, and at once set to work to consult the stars. The cousin's son was a nice-looking, well-grown young fellow, had never been shaved, and had never worn boots. True, he had been a Jumping Jack for a Christmas or two in his earlier days, but there was scarcely any trace of this discoverable about him, his appearance had been so altered by his father's care. He had appeared last Christmas in a beautiful red coat with gold trimmings, a sword by his side, his hat under his arm, and a fine wig with a pigtail. Thus apparelled, he stood in his father's shop exceedingly lovely to behold, and from his native *galanterie* he occupied himself in cracking nuts for the young ladies, who called him "the handsome nutcracker."

Next morning the Astronomer fell, with much emotion, into the Arcanist's arms, crying:

"This is the very man!—we have him!—he is found! Only, dearest colleague, two things we must keep carefully in view. In the first place, we must construct a most substantial pigtail for this precious nephew of yours, which shall be connected with his lower jaw in such sort that it shall be capable of communicating a very powerful pull to it. And next, when we get back to the Residenz, we must carefully conceal the fact that we have brought the young gentleman who is to shiver the nut back with us. He must not make his appearance for a considerable time after us. I read in the horoscope that if two or three others bite at the nut unsuccessfully to begin with, the king will promise the man who breaks it—and as a consequence, restores her good looks to the princess—the princess's hand and the succession to the crown.''

The doll-maker cousin was immensely delighted with the idea of his son's marrying Princess Pirlipat and being a prince and king, so he gave him wholly over to the envoys to do what they liked with him. The pigtail which Drosselmeier attached to him proved to be a very powerful and efficient instrument, as he exemplified by cracking the hardest of peach-stones with the utmost ease.

Drosselmeier and the Astronomer, having at once sent news to the Residenz of the discovery of the nut Crackatook, the necessary advertisements were at once put in the newspapers, and by the time that our travellers got there, several nice young gentlemen had arrived, among whom there were even princes, who had sufficient confidence in their teeth to try to disenchant the princess. The ambassadors were horrified when they saw poor Pirlipat again. The diminutive body with tiny hands and feet was not big enough to support the great shapeless head. The hideousness of the face was enhanced by a beard like white cotton, which had grown about the mouth and chin. Everything had turned out as the court astronomer had read it in the horoscope. One milksop in shoes after another bit his teeth and his jaws into agonies over the nut without doing the princess the slightest good in the world. And then, when he was carried out on the verge of insensibility by the dentists who were in attendance on purpose, he would sigh:

"Ah dear, that *was* a hard nut."

Now when the king, in the anguish of his soul, had promised to him who should disenchant the princess his daughter and the kingdom, the charming, gentle young Drosselmeier made his appearance, and begged to be allowed to make an attempt. None of the previous ones had pleased the princess so much. She pressed her little hands to her heart and sighed:

"Ah, I hope it will be he who will crack the nut and be my husband."

When he had politely saluted the king, the queen, and the Princess Pirlipat, he received the nut Crackatook from the hands of the Clerk of the Closet, put it between his teeth, made a strong effort with his head, and—crack—crack—the shell was shattered into a number of pieces. He neatly cleared the kernel from the pieces of husk which were sticking to it, and making a leg presented it courteously to the princess, after which he closed his eyes and began his backward steps. The princess swallowed the kernel, and—oh marvel!—the monstrosity vanished, and in its place there stood a wonderfully beautiful lady with a face which seemed woven of delicate lily-white and rose-red silk, eyes of sparkling azure, and hair all in little curls like threads of gold.

Trumpets and kettledrums mingled in the loud rejoicings of the populace. The king and all his court danced about on one leg, as they had done at Pirlipat's birth, and the queen had to be treated with Eau de Cologne, having fallen into a fainting fit from joy and delight. All this tremendous tumult interfered not a little with young Drosselmeier's self-possession, for he still had to make his seven backward steps. But he collected himself as best he could, and was just stretching out his right foot to make his seventh step, when up came Dame Mouserink through the floor, making a horrible weaking and squeaking, so that Drosselmeier, as he was putting his foot down, trod upon her and stumbled so that he almost fell. Oh misery!—all in an instant he was transmogrified, just as the princess had been before: his body all shrivelled up, and could scarcely support the great shapeless head with enormous projecting eyes and the wide gaping mouth. In the place where his pigtail used to be a scanty wooden cloak hung down, controlling the movements of his nether jaw.

The clockmaker and the astronomer were wild with terror and consternation, but they saw that Dame Mouserink was wallowing in her gore on the floor. Her wickedness had not escaped punishment, for young Drosselmeier had squashed her so in the throat with the sharp point of his shoe that she was mortally hurt.

But as Dame Mouserink lay in her death agony she squeaked and cheeped lamentably and cried:

"Oh, Crackatook, thou nut so hard!—Oh, fate, which none may disregard!—Hee hee, pee pee, woe's me, I cry!—since I through that hard nut must die.—But, brave young Nutcracker, I see—you soon must follow after me.—My sweet young son, with sevenfold crown—will soon bring Master Cracker down.—His mother's death he will repay—so, Nutcracker, beware that day!—Oh, life most sweet, I feebly cry—I leave you now, for I must die. Queak!"

With this cry died Dame Mouserink, and her body was carried out by the Court Stovelighter. Meantime nobody had been troubling himself about young Drosselmeier. But the princess reminded the king of his promise, and he at once directed that the young hero should be conducted to his presence. But when the poor wretch came forward in his transmogrified condition the princess put both her hands to her face, and cried:

"Oh please take away that horrid Nutcracker!"

The Lord Chamberlain seized him immediately by his little shoulders, and shied him out at the door. The king, furious at the idea of a nutcracker being brought before him as a son-in-law, laid all the blame upon the clockmaker and the astronomer, and ordered them both to be banished for ever.

The horoscope which the astronomer had drawn in Nuremberg had said nothing about this; but that didn't hinder him from taking some fresh observations. And the stars told him that young Drosselmeier would conduct himself so admirably in his new condition that he would still be a prince and a king, in spite of his transmogrification; but also that his deformity would only disappear after the son of Dame Mouserink, the seven-headed king of the mice (whom she had borne after the death of her original seven sons) should perish by his hand, and a lady should fall in love with him notwithstanding his deformity.

That is the story of the hard nut, children, and now you know why people so often use the expression "that was a hard nut to crack," and why Nutcrackers are so ugly.

Thus did Godpapa Drosselmeier finish his tale. Marie thought the Princess Pirlipat was a nasty ungrateful thing. Fritz, on the other hand, was of the opinion that if Nutcracker had been a proper sort of fellow he would soon have settled the Mouse-King's hash, and got his good looks back again.

UNCLE AND NEPHEW

Should any of my respected readers or listeners ever have happened to be cut by glass they will know what an exceedingly nasty thing it is, and how long it takes to heal. Marie was obliged to stay in bed a whole week because she felt so terribly giddy whenever she tried to stand up; but at last she was quite well again, and able to jump about as of old. Things in the glass cupboard looked very fine indeed —everything new and shiny, trees and flowers and houses—toys of every kind. Above all, Marie found her dear Nutcracker again, smiling at her in the second shelf, with his teeth all sound and right.

As she looked at this pet of hers with much fondness, it suddenly struck her that all Godpapa Drosselmeier's story had been about

Nutcracker, and his family feud with Dame Mouserink and her people. And now she knew that her Nutcracker was none other than young Mr. Drosselmeier, of Nuremberg, Godpapa Drosselmeier's delightful nephew, unfortunately under the spells of Dame Mouserink. For while the story was being told, Marie couldn't doubt for a moment that the clever clockmaker at Pirlipat's father's court was Godpapa Drosselmeier himself.

"But why didn't your uncle help you? Why didn't he help you?" Marie cried, sorrowfully, as she felt more and more clearly every moment that in the battle which she had witnessed the question in dispute had been no less a matter than Nutcracker's crown and kingdom. Weren't all the other toys his subjects? And wasn't it clear that the astronomer's prophecy that he was to be rightful King of Toyland had come true?

While the clever Marie was weighing all these things in her mind, she kept expecting that Nutcracker and his vassals would give some indications of being alive, and make some movements as she looked at them. This, however, was by no means the case. Everything in the cupboard kept quite motionless and still. Marie thought this was the effect of Dame Mouserink's enchantments, and those of her seven-headed son, which still were keeping up their power.

"But," she said, "though you're not able to move, or to say the least little word to me, dear Mr. Drosselmeier, I know you understand me and see how very well I wish you. Always reckon on my assistance when you require it. At all events, I will ask your uncle to aid you with all his great skill and talents, whenever there may be an opportunity."

Nutcracker still kept quiet and motionless. But Marie fancied that a gentle sigh came breathing through the glass cupboard, which made its panes ring in a wonderful, though all but imperceptible, manner—while something like a little bell-toned voice seemed to sing:

"Marie fine, angel mine! I will be thine, if thou wilt be mine!"

Although a sort of cold shiver ran through her at this, still it caused her the keenest pleasure.

Twilight came on. Marie's father came in with Godpapa Drosselmeier, and presently Louise set out the tea-table, and the family took their places round it, talking in the pleasantest and merriest manner about all sorts of things. Marie had taken her little stool, and sat down at her godpapa's feet in silence. When everybody happened to cease talking at the same time, Marie looked her godpapa full in the face with her great blue eyes, and said:

"I know now, godpapa, that my Nutcracker is your nephew, young Mr. Drosselmeier from Nuremberg. The prophecy has come true: he is a king and a prince just as your friend the astronomer said he would be. But you know as well as I do that he is at war with Dame Mouserink's son—that horrid king of the mice. Why don't you help him?"

Marie told the whole story of the battle, as she had witnessed it, and was frequently interrupted by the loud laughter of her mother and sister; but Fritz and Drosselmeier listened quite gravely.

"Where in the name of goodness has the child got her head filled with all that nonsense?" cried her father.

"She has such a lively imagination, you see," said her mother; "she dreamt it all when she was feverish with her arm."

"It is all nonsense," cried Fritz, "and it isn't true! My red hussars are not such cowards as all that. If they were, do you suppose I should command them?"

But godpapa smiled strangely, and took little Marie on his knee, speaking more gently to her than ever he had been known to do before.

"More is given to you, Marie dear," he said, "than to me, or the others. You are a born princess, like Pirlipat, and reign in a bright beautiful country. But you still have much to suffer, if you mean to befriend poor transformed Nutcracker; for the king of the mice lies in wait for him at every turn. But I cannot help him; you, and you alone, can do that. So be faithful and true."

Neither Marie nor any of the others knew what Godpapa Drosselmeier meant by these words. But they struck Dr. Stahlbaum—Marie's father—as being so strange that he felt Drosselmeier's pulse, and said:

"There seems a good deal of congestion about the head, my dear sir. I'll write you a little prescription."

But Marie's mother shook her head meditatively, and said:

"I have a strong idea what Mr. Drosselmeier means, though I can't exactly put it in words."

VICTORY

It was not very long before Marie was awakened one bright moonlight night by a curious noise which came from one of the corners of her room. There was a sound as of small stones being thrown, and rolled here and there; and intermittently there came a horrid cheeping and squeaking.

"Oh, dear me! here come these abominable mice again!" cried Marie in terror, and she wanted to awaken her mother. But the noise suddenly ceased; and she could not move a muscle—for she saw the king of the mice working himself out through a hole in the wall. At last he came into the room, ran about in it, and got onto the little table at the head of her bed with a great jump.

"Hee-hehee!" he cried; "give me your candy! out with your cakes, marzipan and sugar-stick, gingerbread cakes! Don't pause to argue! If yield them you won't, I'll chew up Nutcracker! See if I don't!"

As he cried out these terrible words, he gnashed and chattered his teeth most frightfully, and then made off again through the hole in the wall. This frightened Marie so that she was quite pale in the morning, and so upset that she scarcely could utter a word. A hundred times she felt impelled to tell her mother or her sister, or at all events her brother, what had happened. But she thought, "Of course none of them would believe me. They would only laugh at me."

But she saw well enough that to succour Nutcracker she would have to sacrifice all her sweet things; so she laid out all she had of them at the bottom of the cupboard next evening.

"I can't make out how the mice have got into the sitting-room," said her mother. "This is something quite new. There never were any there before. See, Marie, they've eaten up all your candy."

And so it was: the epicure Mouse-King hadn't found the marzipan altogether to his taste, but had gnawed all round the edges of it, so that what he had left of it had to be thrown into the ash-pit. Marie did not mind about her candy, being delighted to think that she had saved Nutcracker by means of it. But what were her feelings when next night there again came a squeaking close by her ear. Alas! The king of the mice was there again, with his eyes glaring worse than the night before.

"Give me your sugar toys," he cried; "give them you must, or else I'll chew Nutcracker up into dust!"

Then he was gone again.

Marie was very sorry. She had as beautiful a collection of sugar-toys as ever a little girl could boast of. Not only had she a charming little shepherd, with his shepherdess, looking after a flock of milk-white sheep, with a nice dog jumping about them, but two postmen with letters in their hands, and four couples of prettily dressed young gentlemen and most beautifully dressed young ladies, swinging in a Russian swing. Then there were two or three dancers, and behind them Farmer Feldkuemmel and the Maid of Orleans. Marie didn't much care about *them*; but back in the corner there was a little baby with red cheeks, and this was Marie's darling. The tears came to her eyes.

"Ah!" she cried, turning to Nutcracker, "I really will do all I can to help you. But it's very hard."

Nutcracker looked at her so piteously that she determined to sacrifice everything—for she remembered the Mouse-King with all his seven mouths wide open to swallow the poor young fellow; so that night she set down all her sugar figures in front of the cupboard, as she had the candy the night before. She kissed the shepherd, the shepherdess, and the lambs; and at last she brought her best beloved of all, the little red-cheeked baby from its corner, but did put it a little further back than the rest. Farmer Feldkuemmel and the Maid of Orleans had to stand in the front rank.

"This is really getting too bad," said Marie's mother the next morning; "some nasty mouse or other must have made a hole in the glass cupboard, for poor Marie's sugar figures are all eaten and gnawed." Marie really could not restrain her tears. But she was soon able to smile again; for she thought, "What does it matter? Nutcracker is safe."

In the evening Marie's mother was telling her father and Godpapa Drosselmeier about the mischief which some mouse was doing in the children's cupboard, and her father said:

"It's a regular nuisance! What a pity that we can't get rid of it. It's destroying all the poor child's things."

Fritz intervened, and remarked, "The baker downstairs has a fine grey Councillor-of-Legation; I'll go and get hold of him, and he'll soon put a stop to it, and bite the mouse's head off, even if it's Dame Mouserink herself, or her son, the king of the mice."

"Oh, yes!" said his mother, laughing, "and jump up on to the chairs and tables, knock down the cups and glasses, and do ever so much mischief besides."

"No, no!" answered Fritz; "the baker's Councillor-of-Legation's a very clever fellow. I wish I could walk about on the edge of the roof, as he does."

"Don't let us have a nasty cat in the house in the night-time," said Louise, who hated cats.

"Fritz is quite right though," said their mother; "unless we set a trap. Haven't we got such a thing in the house?"

"Godpapa Drosselmeier's the man to get us one," said Fritz; "it was he who invented them, you know." Everybody laughed. And when their mother said they did not possess such a thing, Drosselmeier said he had plenty; and he actually sent a very fine one round that day. When the cook was browning the fat, Marie— with her head full of the marvels of her godpapa's tale—called out to her:

"Ah, take care, Queen! Remember Dame Mouserink and her people." But Fritz drew his sword, and cried, "Let them come if they dare! I'll give an account of them." But everything about the hearth remained quiet and undisturbed. As Drosselmeier was fixing the browned fat on a fine thread, and setting the trap gently down in the glass cupboard, Fritz cried:

"Now, Godpapa Clockmaker, mind that the Mouse-King doesn't play you some trick!"

Ah, how did it fare with Marie that night? Something as cold as ice went tripping about on her arm, and something rough and nasty laid itself on her cheek, and cheeped and squeaked in her ear. The horrible Mouse-King came and sat on her shoulder, foamed a blood-red foam out of all his seven mouths, and chattering and grinding his teeth, he hissed into Marie's ear:

"Hiss, hiss!—keep away—don't go in there—beware of that house—don't you be caught—death to the mouse—hand out your picture books—none of your scornful looks!—Give me your dresses —also your laces—or, if you don't, leave you I won't—Nutcracker I'll bite—drag him out of your sight—his last hour is near—so tremble for fear!—Fee, fa, fo, fum—his last hour is come!—Hee hee, pee pee—squeak—squeak!"

Marie was overwhelmed with anguish and sorrow, and was looking quite pale and upset when her mother said to her next morning:

"This horrid mouse hasn't been caught. But never mind, dear, we'll catch the nasty thing yet, never fear. If the traps won't work, Fritz shall fetch the grey Councillor-of-Legation."

As soon as Marie was alone, she went up to the glass cupboard, and said to Nutcracker, in a voice broken by sobs:

"Ah, my dear, good Mr. Drosselmeier, what can I do for you, poor unfortunate girl that I am! Even if I give that horrid king of the mice all my picture books, and my new dress which the Christ Child gave me at Christmas as well, he's sure to go on asking for more."

Soon I shan't have anything more left, and he'll want to eat *me*! Oh, poor thing that I am! What shall I do? What shall I do?"

As she was thus crying and lamenting, she noticed that a great spot of blood had been left, since the eventful night of the battle, upon Nutcracker's neck. Since she had known that he was really young Mr. Drosselmeier, her godpapa's nephew, she had given up carrying him in her arms, and petting and kissing him; indeed, she felt a delicacy about touching him at all. But now she took him carefully out of his shelf, and began to wipe off this blood spot with her handkerchief. What were her feelings when she found that Nutcracker was growing warmer and warmer in her hand, and beginning to move! She put him back into the cupboard as fast as she could. His mouth began to wobble backwards and forwards, and he began to whisper, with much difficulty:

"Ah, dearest Miss Stahlbaum—most precious of friends! How deeply I am indebted to you for everything—for *everything*! But don't, don't sacrifice any of your picture books or pretty dresses for me. Get me a sword—a sword is what I want. If you get me that, I'll manage the rest—though—he may—"

There Nutcracker's speech died away, and his eyes, which had been expressing the most sympathetic grief, grew staring and lifeless again.

Marie felt no fear; she jumped for joy, rather, now that she knew how to help Nutcracker without further painful sacrifices. But where on earth was she to get hold of a sword for him? She resolved to take counsel with Fritz; and that evening when their father and mother had gone out, and they two were sitting beside the glass cupboard, she told him what had passed between her and Nutcracker with the king of the mice, and what it was that was required to rescue Nutcracker.

The thing which chiefly exercised Fritz's mind was Marie's statement as to the unexemplary conduct of his red hussars in the great battle. He asked her once more, most seriously, to assure him that it really was the truth; and when she had repeated her statement on her word of honour, he advanced to the cupboard and made his hussars a most affecting address. As a punishment for their behaviour, he solemnly took their plumes one by one out of their busbies, and prohibited them from sounding the march of the hussars of the guard for the space of a twelvemonth. When he had performed this duty, he turned to Marie and said:

"As far as the sword is concerned, I have it in my power to assist Nutcracker. I placed an old Colonel of Cuirassiers on retirement on a pension yesterday, so that he has no further occasion for his sabre, which is sharp."

This Colonel was settled, on his pension, in the back corner of the third shelf. He was fetched out and his sabre—still a bright and handsome silver weapon—taken off, and girt about Nutcracker.

Next night Marie could not close an eye for anxiety. About midnight she fancied she heard a strange stirring and noise in the sitting-room—a rustling and a clanging—and suddenly there came a shrill "Queak!"

"The king of the mice! The king of the mice!" she cried, and jumped out of bed, all terror. Everything was silent; but soon there came a gentle tapping at the door of her room, and a soft voice made itself heard, saying:

"Please open your door, dearest Miss Stahlbaum! Don't be in the least degree alarmed; good, happy news!"

It was Drosselmeier's voice—young Drosselmeier's, I mean. She threw on her dressing-gown and opened the door as quickly as possible. There stood Nutcracker, with his sword all covered with blood in his right hand, and a little wax taper in his left. When he saw Marie, he knelt down on one knee, and said:

"It was you, and you only, dearest lady, who inspired me with knightly valour, and steeled me with strength to do battle with the insolent caitiff who dared to insult you. The treacherous king of the mice lies vanquished and writhing in his gore! Deign, lady, to accept these tokens of victory from the hand of him who is, till death, your true and faithful knight."

With this Nutcracker took from his left arm the seven crowns of the Mouse-King, which he had ranged upon it, and handed them to Marie, who received them with the keenest pleasure. Nutcracker rose and continued as follows:

"Oh! my best beloved Miss Stahlbaum, if you would only take the trouble to follow me for a few steps, what glorious and beautiful things I could show you, at this supreme moment when I have overcome my hereditary foe! Do—do come with me, dearest lady!"

TOYLAND

I feel quite convinced, children, that none of you would have hesitated for a moment to go with good, kind Nutcracker, who had always shown himself to be such a charming person, and Marie was all the more disposed to do as he asked her, because she knew what her just claims on his gratitude were, and was sure that he would keep his word, and show her all sorts of beautiful things. So she said:

"I will go with you, dear Mr. Drosselmeier; but it mustn't be very far, and it won't do to be very long, because, you know, I haven't had any sleep yet."

"Then we will go by the shortest route," said Nutcracker, "although it is, perhaps, rather the most difficult."

He went on in front, followed by Marie, till he stopped before the big old wardrobe. Marie was surprised to see that though it was generally shut, the doors of it were now wide open, so that she could see her father's travelling cloak of fox-fur hanging in the front. Nutcracker clambered deftly up this cloak, by the edgings and trimmings of it, so as to get hold of the big tassel which was fastened at the back of it by a thick cord. He gave this tassel a tug, and a pretty little ladder of cedarwood let itself quickly down through one of the armholes of the cloak.

"Now, Miss Stahlbaum, step up that ladder, if you will be so kind," said Nutcracker. Marie did so. But as soon as she had got up through the armhole, and began to look out at the neck, a dazzling light came streaming on her, and she found herself standing on a lovely, sweet-scented meadow, from which millions of sparks were streaming upward, like the glitter of beautiful gems.

"This is Candy Mead, where we are now," said Nutcracker. "But we'll go in at that gate there."

Marie looked up and saw a beautiful gateway on the meadow, only a few steps off. It seemed to be made of white, brown, and raisin-coloured marble; but when she came close to it she saw it was all of baked sugar-almonds and raisins, which—as Nutcracker said when they were going through it—was the reason it was called "Almond and Raisin Gate." There was a gallery running round the upper part of it, apparently made of barley sugar, and in this gallery six monkeys, dressed in red doublets, were playing on brass instruments in the most delightful manner ever heard. It was all that Marie could do to notice that she was walking along upon a beautiful variegated marble pavement, which, however, was really a mosaic of lozenges of all colours. Presently the sweetest of odours came breathing round her, streaming from a beautiful little wood on both sides of the way. There was such a glittering and sparkling among the dark foliage that one could see all the gold and silver fruits hanging on the many-tinted stems, and these stems and branches were all ornamented and dressed up in ribbons and bunches of flowers like brides and bridegrooms and festive wedding guests. And as the orange perfume came wafted, as if on the wings of gentle zephyrs, there was a soughing among the leaves and branches, and all the gold-leaf and tinsel rustled and tinkled like beautiful music, to which the sparkling lights could not help dancing.

"Oh, how charming this is!" cried Marie, enraptured.

"This is Christmas Wood, dearest Miss Stahlbaum," said Nutcracker.

"Ah!" said Marie, "if I could only stay here for a little! Oh, it is so lovely!"

Nutcracker clapped his little hands, and immediately there appeared a number of little shepherds and shepherdesses, and hunters and huntresses, so white and delicate that you would have thought they were made of pure sugar, whom Marie had not noticed before, although they had been walking about in the wood. They brought a beautiful gold reclining chair, laid a white satin cushion in it, and politely invited Marie to take a seat. As soon as she did so, the shepherds and shepherdesses danced a pretty ballet, to which the hunters and huntresses played music on their horns, and then they all disappeared among the thickets.

"I must really apologize for the poor style in which this dance was executed, dearest Miss Stahlbaum," said Nutcracker. "These people all belong to our Wire Ballet Troupe, and can only do the same thing over and over again. Had we not better go on a little farther?"

"Oh, I'm sure it was all most delightful, and I enjoyed it immensely!" said Marie, as she stood up and followed Nutcracker, who was leading the way. They went by the side of a gently rippling brook, which seemed to be what was giving out all the perfume which filled the wood.

"This is Orange Brook," said Nutcracker; "but, except for its sweet scent, it is nowhere nearly as fine a water as the River Lemonade, a beautiful broad stream, which falls—as this one does also—into the Almond-milk Sea."

And, indeed, Marie soon heard a louder plashing and rushing, and came in sight of the River Lemonade, which went rolling along in swelling waves of a yellowish colour, between banks covered with a herbage and underbrush which shone like green carbuncles. A remarkable freshness and coolness, strengthening heart and breast, exhaled from this fine river. Not far from it a dark yellow stream crept sluggishly along, giving out a most delicious odour; and on its banks sat numbers of pretty children, angling for little fat fishes, which they ate as soon as they caught them. These fish were very much like filberts, Marie saw when she came closer. A short distance farther, on the banks of this stream, stood a nice little village. The houses of this village, and the church, the parsonage, the barns, and so forth, were all dark brown with gilt roofs, and many of the walls looked as if they were plastered over with lemon peel and shelled almonds.

"That is Gingerthorpe on the Honey River," said Nutcracker. "It is famed for the good looks of its inhabitants; but they are very short-tempered people, because they suffer so much from toothache. So we won't go there at present."

At this moment Marie caught sight of a little town where the houses were all sorts of colours and quite transparent, exceedingly pretty to look at. Nutcracker went on towards this town, and Marie heard a noise of bustle and merriment, and saw some thousands of nice little folks unloading a number of wagons which were drawn up in the market place. What they were unloading from the wagons looked like packages of coloured paper and tablets of chocolate.

"This is Bonbonville," Nutcracker said. "An embassy has just arrived from Paperland and the King of Chocolate. These poor Bonbonville people have been vexatiously threatened lately by the Fly-Admiral's forces, so they are covering their houses over with their presents from Paperland, and constructing fortifications with the fine pieces of workmanship which the Chocolate-King has sent them. But oh! dearest Miss Stahlbaum, we are not going to restrict ourselves to seeing the small towns and villages of this country. Let us be off to the metropolis."

He stepped quickly onwards, and Marie followed him, all expectation. Soon a beautiful rosy vapour began to rise, suffusing everything with a soft splendour. She saw that this was reflected from rose-red, shining water, which went plashing and rushing away in front of them in wavelets of roseate silver. And on this delightful water, which kept broadening and broadening out wider and wider, like a great lake, the loveliest swans were floating, white as silver, with collars of gold. And, as if vying with each other, they were singing the most beautiful songs, at which little fish, glittering like diamonds, danced up and down in the rosy ripples.

"Oh!" cried Marie, in the greatest delight, "this must be the lake which Godpapa Drosselmeier was once going to make for me, and I am the girl who is to play with the swans."

Nutcracker gave a sneering sort of laugh, such as she had never seen in him before, and said:

"My uncle could never make a thing of this kind. You would be much more likely to do it yourself. But don't let us bother about that. Rather let us go sailing over the water, Lake Rosa here, to the metropolis."

THE METROPOLIS

Nutcracker clapped his little hands again, and the waves of Lake Rosa began to sound louder and to splash higher, and Marie became aware of a sort of car approaching from the distance, made wholly of glittering precious stones of every colour, and drawn by two dolphins with scales of gold. Twelve of the dearest little Negro boys, with headdresses and doublets made of hummingbirds' feathers woven together, jumped to land, and carried first Marie and then Nutcracker, gently gliding above the water, into the car, which immediately began to move along over the lake of its own accord. Ah! how beautiful it was when Marie went over the waters in the shell-shaped car, with the rose-perfume breathing around her, and the rosy waves splashing. The two golden-scaled dolphins lifted their nostrils, and sent streams of crystal high in the air; and as these fell down in glittering, sparkling rainbows, there was a sound as of two delicate, silvery voices, singing, "Who comes over the rosy sea?—Fairy is she. Bim-bim—fishes; sim-sim—swans; sfa-sfa— golden birds; tratrah, rosy waves, wake you, and sing, sparkle and ring, sprinkle and kling—this is the fairy we languish to see— coming at last to us over the sea. Rosy waves dash—bright dolphins play—merrily, merrily on!"

But the twelve little boys at the back of the car seemed to take some umbrage at this song of the water jets; for they shook the sun shades they were holding so that the palm leaves they were made of clattered and rattled together; and as they shook them they stamped an odd sort of rhythm with their feet, and sang:

"Klapp and klipp, and klipp and klapp, and up and down."

"These are merry, amusing fellows," said Nutcracker, a little put out, "but they'll set the whole lake into a state of regular mutiny on my hands!" And in fact there did begin a confused and confusing noise of strange voices which seemed to be floating both in the water and in the air. However, Marie paid no attention to it, but went on looking into the perfumed rosy waves, from each of which a pretty girl's face smiled back to her.

"Oh! look at Princess Pirlipat," she cried, clapping her hands with gladness, "smiling at me so charmingly down there! Do look at her, Mr. Drosselmeier."

But Nutcracker sighed, almost sorrowfully, and said:

"That is not Princess Pirlipat, dearest Miss Stahlbaum, it is only yourself; always your own lovely face smiling up from the rosy waves." At this Marie drew her head quickly back, closed her eyes as tightly as she could, and was terribly ashamed. But just then the twelve Negroes lifted her out of the car and set her on shore. She found herself in a small thicket or grove, almost more beautiful even than Christmas Wood, everything glittered and sparkled so in it. And the fruit on the trees was extraordinarily wonderful and beautiful, and not only of very curious colours, but with the most delicious perfume.

"Ah!" said Nutcracker, "here we are in Comfit Grove, and yonder lies the metropolis."

How shall I set about describing all the wonderful and beautiful sights which Marie now saw, or give any idea of the splendour and magnificence of the city which lay stretched out before her on a flowery plain? Not only did the walls and towers of it shine in the brightest and most gorgeous colours, but the shapes and appearance of the buildings were like nothing to be seen on earth. Instead of roofs the houses had on beautiful twining crowns, and the towers were garlanded with beautiful leaf-work, sculptured and carved into exquisite, intricate designs. As they passed in at the gateway, which looked as if it was made entirely of macaroons and sugared fruits, silver soldiers presented arms, and a little man in a brocade dressing gown threw himself upon Nutcracker's neck, crying:

"Welcome, dearest prince! welcome to Sweetmeatburgh!"

Marie wondered not a little to see such a very grand personage recognize young Mr. Drosselmeier as a prince. But she heard such a number of small delicate voices making such a loud clamouring and talking, and such a laughing and chattering going on, and such a singing and playing, that she couldn't give her attention to anything else, but asked Drosselmeier what was the meaning of it all.

"Oh, it is nothing out of the common, dearest Miss Stahlbaum," he answered. "Sweetmeatburgh is a large, populous city, full of mirth and entertainment. This is only the usual thing that is always going on here every day. Please come on a little farther."

After a few paces more they were in the great market place, which presented the most magnificent appearance. All the houses which were round it were of filagreed sugarwork, with galleries towering above galleries; and in the centre stood a lofty cake covered with sugar, by way of obelisk, with fountains round it spouting orgeat, lemonade, and other delicious beverages into the air. The runnels at the sides of the footways were full of creams, which you might have ladled up with a spoon if you had chosen. But prettier than all this were the delightful little people who were crowding about everywhere by the thousand, shouting, laughing, playing, and singing, in short, producing all that jubilant uproar which Marie had heard from the distance. There were beautifully dressed ladies and gentlemen, Greeks and Armenians, Tyrolese and Jews, officers and soldiers, clergymen, shepherds, jack-puddings, in short, people of every conceivable kind to be found in the world.

The tumult grew greater towards one of the corners; the people streamed asunder. For the Great Mogul happened to be passing along there in his palanquin, attended by three-and-ninety grandees of the realm, and seven hundred slaves. But it chanced that the Fishermen's Guild, about five hundred strong, were keeping a festival at the opposite corner of the place; and it was rather an unfortunate coincidence that the Grand Turk took it in his head just at this particular moment to go out for a ride, and crossed the square with three thousand Janissaries. And, as if this were not enough, the grand procession of the Interrupted Sacrifice came along at the same time, marching up towards the obelisk with a full orchestra playing, and the chorus singing: "Hail! all hail to the glorious sun!"

So there was a thronging and a shoving, a driving and a squeaking; and soon lamentations arose, and cries of pain, for one of the fishermen had knocked a Brahmin's head off in the throng, and the Great Mogul had been very nearly run down by a jack-pudding. The din grew wilder and wilder. People were beginning to shove one another, and even to come to fisticuffs; when the man in the brocade dressing gown who had welcomed Nutcracker as prince at the gate, clambered up to the top of the obelisk, and, after a very clear-tinkling bell had rung thrice, shouted very loudly three times: "Pastrycook! pastrycook! pastrycook!"

Instantly the tumult subsided. Everybody tried to save himself as quickly as he could; and after the entangled processions had been disentangled, the dirt properly brushed off the Great Mogul, and the Brahmin's head stuck on again all right, the merry noise went on just the same as before.

"Tell me why that gentleman called out 'Pastrycook,' Mr. Drosselmeier, please," said Marie.

"Ah! dearest Miss Stahlbaum," said Nutcracker, "in this place 'Pastrycook' means a certain unknown and very terrible Power, which it is believed can do with people just what it chooses. It represents the Fate or Destiny which rules these happy little people, and they stand in such awe and terror of it that the mere mention of its name quells the wildest tumult in a moment, as the burgomaster has just shown. Nobody thinks further of earthly matters, cuffs in the ribs, broken heads, or the like. Every one retires within himself, and says: 'What is man? and what his ultimate destiny?'"

Marie could not forbear a cry of admiration and utmost astonishment as she now found herself suddenly before a castle shining in roseate radiance, with a hundred beautiful towers. Here and there at intervals upon its walls were rich bouquets of violets, narcissuses, tulips, carnations, whose dark, glowing colours heightened the dazzling whiteness, inclining to rose-colour, of the walls. The great dome of the central building, as well as the pyramidal roofs of the towers, were set all over with thousands of sparkling gold and silver stars.

"Aha!" said Nutcracker, "here we are at Marzipan Castle at last!"

Marie was sunk and absorbed in contemplation of this magic palace. But the fact did not escape her that the roof was wanting to one of the principal towers, and that little men up upon a scaffold made of sticks of cinnamon were busy putting it on again. But before she had had time to ask Nutcracker about this, he said:

"This beautiful castle a short time ago was threatened with tremendous havoc, if not with total destruction. Sweet-tooth the giant happened to be passing by, and he bit off the top of that tower there, and was beginning to gnaw at the great dome. But the Sweetmeatburgh people brought him a whole quarter of the town by way of tribute, and a considerable slice of Comfit Grove into the bargain. This stopped his mouth, and he went on his way."

At this moment, soft, beautiful music was heard, and out came twelve little pages with lighted clove-sticks, which they held in their little hands by way of torches. Each of their heads was a pearl, their bodies were emeralds and rubies, and their feet were beautifully worked pure gold. After them came four ladies about the size of Marie's Miss Clara, but so gloriously and brilliantly attired that Marie saw in a moment that they could be nothing but princesses of the blood royal. They embraced Nutcracker most tenderly, and shed tears of gladness, saying, "Oh, dearest prince! beloved brother!"

Nutcracker seemed deeply affected. He wiped away his tears, which flowed thick and fast, and then he took Marie by the hand and said with much pathos and solemnity:

"This is Miss Marie Stahlbaum, the daughter of a most worthy medical man and the preserver of my life. Had she not thrown her slipper just in the nick of time—had she not procured me the pensioned Colonel's sword—I should have been lying in my cold grave at this moment, bitten to death by the accursed king of the mice. I ask you to tell me candidly, can Princess Pirlipat, princess though she is, compare for a moment with Miss Stahlbaum here in beauty, in goodness, in virtues of every kind? My answer is, emphatically 'No.'"

All the ladies cried "No;" and they fell upon Marie's neck with sobs and tears, and cried: "Ah! noble preserver of our beloved royal brother! Excellent Miss Stahlbaum!"

They now conducted Marie and Nutcracker into the castle, to a hall whose walls were composed of sparkling crystal. But what delighted Marie most of all was the furniture. There were the most darling little chairs, bureaus, writing-tables, and so forth, standing about everywhere, all made of cedar or Brazil-wood, covered with golden flowers. The princesses made Marie and Nutcracker sit down, and said that they would themselves prepare a banquet. So they went and brought quantities of little cups and dishes of the finest Japanese porcelain, and spoons, knives and forks, graters and stew pans, and other kitchen utensils of gold and silver. Then they fetched the most delightful fruits and sugar things—such as Marie had never seen the like of—and began to squeeze the fruit in the daintiest way with their little hands, and to grate the spices and rub down the sugar-almonds; in short, they set to work so skillfully that Marie could see very well how accomplished they were in kitchen matters, and what a magnificent banquet there was going to be. Knowing her own skill in this line, she wished in her secret heart, that she might be allowed to go and help the princesses and have a finger in all these pies herself. And the prettiest of Nutcracker's sisters, just as if she had read the wishes of Marie's heart, handed her a little gold mortar, saying:

"Sweet friend, dear preserver of my brother, would you mind pounding a little of this sugar-candy?"

Now as Marie went on pounding in the mortar with good will and the utmost enjoyment—and the sound of it was like a lovely song—Nutcracker began to relate with much minuteness all that had happened on the occasion of the terrible engagement between his forces and the army of the king of the mice; how he had had the worst of it on account of the bad behaviour of his troops; how the horrible mouse king had all but bitten him to death, so that Marie had had to sacrifice a number of his subjects who were in her service, etc., etc.

During all this it seemed to Marie as if what Nutcracker was saying—and even the sound of her own mortar—kept growing more and more indistinct, and going farther and farther away. Presently she saw a silver mistiness rising up all about, like clouds, in which the princesses, the pages, Nutcracker, and she herself were floating. And a curious singing and a buzzing and humming began, which seemed to die away in the distance; and then she seemed to be going up—up—up, as if on waves constantly rising and swelling higher and higher, higher and higher, higher and higher.

CONCLUSION

And then came a "prr-poof," and Marie fell down from some inconceivable height.

That was a crash and a tumble!

However, she opened her eyes, and, lo and behold, there she was in her own bed! It was broad daylight, and her mother was standing at her bedside, saying:

"Well, what a sleep you have had! Breakfast has been ready for ever so long."

Of course, dear audience, you see how it was. Marie, confounded and amazed by all the wonderful things she had seen, had at last fallen asleep in Marzipan Castle, and the Negroes or the pages, or perhaps the princesses themselves, had carried her home and put her to bed.

"Oh, mother darling," said Marie, "what a number of places young Mr. Drosselmeier has taken me to in the night, and what beautiful things I have seen!" And she gave very much the same faithful account of it all as I have given to you.

Her mother listened, looking at her with astonishment, and when she had finished, said:

"You have had a long, beautiful dream, Marie; but now you must put it all out of your head."

Marie firmly maintained that she had not been dreaming at all; so her mother took her to the glass cupboard, lifted out Nutcracker from his usual position on the third shelf, and said:

"You silly girl, how can you believe that this wooden figure can have life and motion?"

"Ah, mother," answered Marie, "I know perfectly well that Nutcracker is young Mr. Drosselmeier from Nuremberg, Godpapa Drosselmeier's nephew."

Her father and mother both burst out into laughter.

"It's all very well your laughing at poor Nutcracker, father," cried Marie, almost weeping, "but he spoke very highly of *you*; for when we arrived at Marzipan Castle, and he was introducing me to his sisters, the princesses, he said you were a most worthy medical man."

The laughter grew louder, and Louise and even Fritz joined in it. Marie ran into the next room, took the Mouse-King's seven crowns from her little box, and handed them to her mother, saying, "Look there, then, dear mother; those are the Mouse-King's seven crowns which young Mr. Drosselmeier gave me last night as a proof that he had got the victory."

Her mother gazed in amazement at the little crowns, which were made of some very brilliant, wholly unknown metal, and worked more beautifully than any human hands could have worked them. Dr. Stahlbaum could not cease looking at them with admiration and astonishment either, and both the father and the mother enjoined Marie most earnestly to tell them where she really had got them from. But she could only repeat what she had said before; and when her father scolded her and accused her of untruthfulness, she began to cry bitterly, and said, "Oh, dear me; what can I tell you except the truth!"

At this moment the door opened, and Godpapa Drosselmeier came in, crying, "Hullo! hullo! what's all this? My little Marie crying? What's all this? what's all this?"

Dr. Stahlbaum told him all about it, and showed him the crowns. As soon as he had looked at them, however, he cried out:

"Stuff and nonsense! stuff and nonsense! These are the crowns I used to wear on my watch-chain. I gave them as a present to Marie on her second birthday. Do you mean to tell me you don't remember?"

None of them *did* remember anything of the kind. But Marie, seeing that her father and mother's faces were clear of clouds again, ran up to her godpapa, crying:

"You know all about the affair, Godpapa Drosselmeier; tell it to them. Let them know from your own lips that my Nutcracker is your nephew, young Mr. Drosselmeier from Nuremberg, and that it was he who gave me the crowns." But Drosselmeier made a very angry face, and muttered, "Stupid stuff and nonsense!" upon which Marie's father took her in front of him, and said with much earnestness:

"Now look here, Marie; let there be an end of all this foolish trash and absurd nonsense for once and for all; I'm not going to allow any more of it; and if ever I hear you say again that that idiotic, misshapen Nutcracker is your godpapa's nephew, I shall throw, not only Nutcracker, but all your other playthings—Miss Clara not excepted—out of the window."

Of course poor Marie dared not utter another word concerning that which her whole mind was full of, for you may well suppose that it was impossible for anyone who had seen all that she had seen to forget it. And I regret to say that even Fritz himself at once turned his back on his sister whenever she wanted to talk to him about the wondrous realm in which she had been so happy. Indeed, he is said to have frequently murmured, "Stupid goose!" between his teeth, though I can scarcely think this compatible with his proved kindness of heart. This much, however, is matter of certainty, that as he no longer believed what his sister said, he now at a public parade formally recanted what he had said to his red hussars, and in the place of the plumes he had deprived them of, gave them much taller and finer ones of goose quills and allowed them to sound the march of the hussars of the guard as before.

Marie did not dare to say anything more of her adventures. But the memories of that fairy realm haunted her with a sweet intoxication, and the music of that delightful, happy country still rang sweetly in her ears. Whenever she allowed her thoughts to dwell on all those glories, she saw them again, and so it came about that, instead of playing as she used to, she sat quiet and meditative, absorbed within herself. Everybody found fault with her for being such a little dreamer.

It chanced one day that Godpapa Drosselmeier was repairing one of the clocks in the house, and Marie was sitting beside the glass cupboard, sunk in her dreams and gazing at Nutcracker. All at once she said, as if involuntarily:

"Ah, dear Mr. Drosselmeier, if you really were alive, *I* shouldn't be like Princess Pirlipat and despise you because you had had to give up being a nice handsome gentleman for my sake!"

"Stupid stuff and nonsense!" cried Godpapa Drosselmeier.

But, as he spoke, there came such a tremendous bang and shock that Marie fell from her chair insensible.

When she came back to her senses her mother was busied about her and said, "How could you go and tumble off your chair in that way, a big girl like you? Here is Godpapa Drosselmeier's nephew come from Nuremberg. See how good you can be."

Marie looked up. Her godpapa had on his yellow coat and his glass wig, and was smiling in the highest good humour. By the hand he was holding a very small but very handsome young gentleman. His little face was red and white; he had on a beautiful red coat trimmed with gold lace, white silk stockings and shoes, with a lovely bouquet of flowers in his shirt frill. He was beautifully frizzed and powdered, and had a magnificent queue hanging down his back. The little sword at his side seemed to be made entirely of jewels, it sparkled and shone so, and the little hat under his arm was woven of flocks of silk. He gave proof of the fineness of his manners in that he had brought for Marie a quantity of the most delightful toys—above all, the very same figures as those which the Mouse-King had eaten up—as well as a beautiful sabre for Fritz. He cracked nuts at table for the whole party; the very hardest did not withstand him. He placed them in his mouth with his left hand, tugged at his pigtail with his right, and crack! they fell in pieces.

Marie grew red as a rose at the sight of this charming young gentleman; and she grew redder still when after dinner young Drosselmeier asked her to go with him to the glass cupboard in the sitting-room.

"Play nicely together, children," said Godpapa Drosselmeier; "now that my clocks are all nicely in order, I can have no possible objection."

But as soon as young Drosselmeier was alone with Marie, he went down on one knee, and spoke as follows:

"Ah! my most dearly beloved Miss Stahlbaum! see here at your feet the fortunate Drosselmeier, whose life you saved here on this very spot. You were kind enough to say, plainly and unmistakably, in so many words, that *you* would not have despised me, as Princess Pirlipat did, if I had been turned ugly for your sake. Immediately I ceased to be a contemptible Nutcracker, and resumed my former not altogether ill-looking person and form. Ah! most exquisite lady! bless me with your precious hand; share with me my crown and kingdom, and reign with me in Marzipan Castle, for there I am now king."

Marie raised him, and said gently, "Dear Mr. Drosselmeier, you are a kind, nice gentleman; and as you reign over a delightful country of charming, funny, pretty people, I accept your hand."

So then they were formally betrothed; and when a year and a day had come and gone, they say he came and fetched her away in a golden coach, drawn by silver horses. At the marriage there danced two-and-twenty thousand of the most beautiful dolls and other figures, all glittering in pearls and diamonds; and Marie is to this day the queen of a realm where all kinds of sparkling Christmas Woods, and transparent Marzipan Castles—in short, the most wonderful and beautiful things of every kind—are to be seen—by those who have the eyes to see them.

So this is the end of the tale of Nutcracker and the King of the Mice.

DOVER·THRIFT·EDITIONS

All books complete and unabridged. All 5³⁄₁₆″ × 8¼″, paperbound.
Just $1.00 each in U.S.A.

FICTION

FLATLAND: A ROMANCE OF MANY DIMENSIONS, Edwin A. Abbott. 96pp. 27263-X

BEOWULF, Beowulf (trans. by R. K. Gordon). 64pp. 27264-8

ALICE'S ADVENTURES IN WONDERLAND, Lewis Carroll. 96pp. 27543-4

O PIONEERS!, Willa Cather. 128pp. 27785-2

FIVE GREAT SHORT STORIES, Anton Chekhov. 96pp. 26463-7

FAVORITE FATHER BROWN STORIES, G. K. Chesterton. 96pp. 27545-0

THE AWAKENING, Kate Chopin. 128pp. 27786-0

HEART OF DARKNESS, Joseph Conrad. 80pp. 26464-5

THE SECRET SHARER AND OTHER STORIES, Joseph Conrad. 128pp. 27546-9

THE OPEN BOAT AND OTHER STORIES, Stephen Crane. 128pp. 27547-7

THE RED BADGE OF COURAGE, Stephen Crane. 112pp. 26465-3

A CHRISTMAS CAROL, Charles Dickens. 80pp. 26865-9

NOTES FROM THE UNDERGROUND, Fyodor Dostoyevsky. 96pp. 27053-X

SIX GREAT SHERLOCK HOLMES STORIES, Sir Arthur Conan Doyle. 112pp. 27055-6

WHERE ANGELS FEAR TO TREAD, E. M. Forster. 128pp. (Available in U.S. only) 27791-7

THE OVERCOAT AND OTHER SHORT STORIES, Nikolai Gogol. 112pp. 27057-2

GREAT GHOST STORIES, John Grafton (ed.). 112pp. 27270-2

THE LUCK OF ROARING CAMP AND OTHER SHORT STORIES, Bret Harte. 96pp. 27271-0

YOUNG GOODMAN BROWN AND OTHER SHORT STORIES, Nathaniel Hawthorne. 128pp. 27060-2

THE GIFT OF THE MAGI AND OTHER SHORT STORIES, O. Henry. 96pp. 27061-0

THE NUTCRACKER AND THE GOLDEN POT, E. T. A. Hoffmann. 128pp. 27806-9

THE BEAST IN THE JUNGLE AND OTHER STORIES, Henry James. 128pp. 27552-3

THE TURN OF THE SCREW, Henry James. 96pp. 26684-2

DUBLINERS, James Joyce. 160pp. 26870-5

SELECTED SHORT STORIES, D. H. Lawrence. 128pp. 27794-1

GREEN TEA AND OTHER GHOST STORIES, J. Sheridan LeFanu. 96pp. 27795-X

THE CALL OF THE WILD, Jack London. 64pp. 26472-6

FIVE GREAT SHORT STORIES, Jack London. 96pp. 27063-7

WHITE FANG, Jack London. 160pp. 26968-X

THE NECKLACE AND OTHER SHORT STORIES, Guy de Maupassant. 128pp. 27064-5

BARTLEBY AND BENITO CERENO, Herman Melville. 112pp. 26473-4

THE GOLD-BUG AND OTHER TALES, Edgar Allan Poe. 128pp. 26875-6

THE STRANGE CASE OF DR. JEKYLL AND MR. HYDE, Robert Louis Stevenson. 64pp. 26688-5

TREASURE ISLAND, Robert Louis Stevenson. 160pp. 27559-0

THE KREUTZER SONATA AND OTHER SHORT STORIES, Leo Tolstoy. 144pp. 27805-0

THE MYSTERIOUS STRANGER AND OTHER STORIES, Mark Twain. 128pp. 27069-6